I0685494

GUILTY OF SIN

This book is for entertainment purposes only. Life's stories are real but war stories are just that……

War stories.

Whether right or wrong, fact or fiction, short termed or sentenced to life,, Brothers that fend together stand together.

I want to dedicate this book to my wife, Tesheema Unique York It's said that if you cut loose someone you truly love and by fate you find each other again, it becomes, New beginnings, and a dream that has become reality. To my Mother, Father, and the late Great Charles Miller, I am truly thankful, grateful, and blessed. You counted me in when everyone else counted me out. In life sometimes we take chances for all the wrong reasons; or just make the wrong choices, I choose you, today, tomorrow, and forever, because failure is not an option. 2/28/14

GUILTY OF SIN

A work of Fiction

Rasul York

ISBN: 0692449337
ISBN 13: 9780692449332
Library of Congress Control Number: 2015907887
Rasul York, Paterson, NJ

MIAMI. DADE COUNTY, 11:45PM

"Pointing to a couple empty parking spaces, "this time keep it running, "Yo pull over right here," I swear that look like dude right there". He pointed to what looked like a middle aged, well built, Cuban guy with a salt and pepper pony tail, whom just lit and quickly started puffing on what looked like a thick cigar "Man if that's him," he looked at his driver, at him once again, then looked down at the pictures that were given to him two days ago in almost disbelief, because this was the fourth location and possibly the last one before they started over in the morning, after already driving around the 305 area practically since they arrived there about 1:30 this afternoon. He sighed, squinted his eyes for a better look then spoke, never really taking his eyes off of that ponytail that now has his back to them.

"You know once I put this work in, it'll put us where we need to be..."

I feel you but.. you said you were done with this type ish, bruh."

"I feel you bro, but this opportunity knocked at what couldn't have been a better time, 75Gs. Seven five, there was no way I could turn that down and I won't be the only one to benefit from this, Damn.. I'm giving you twenty five just to ride. I've been trying my best with this honest life since I been home, and every time I feel like I'm up, something kicks me back down the damn stairs."

"Naw 'Red', you missing my point. You know you my man, right?" Just as he was about to finish talking. Rasul with a quick "Shhhh" jester said, "hold that thought."

Putting his finger to his mouth and with his left hand. He opened the front passenger door and slid out all in one motion. All Hollywood could do was watch as they looked each other in the eye while his child hood friend quickly but swiftly opened then closed the door pulling the hoodie above and over his head, then pulled the draw strings as he crossed the street. Three flashes of what sounded like soft thumps of someone knocking on a solid wood door came from his man's left hand.

"Damn I was kind of hoping I could've talked him out of this, guess something's we just can't let go." His thoughts raced into a small cloud that could've paired his judgment, Anything could have happened because didn't even realize his boy was already back in the SUV.

"Drive! Drive Wood. Drive!" Wood swiftly shifting into gear, pulling out of the parking space, that they weren't even parked in. His thoughts were still racing but coming back into focus. Sul slipped the hoodie off over his head, stuffing it into a black Swiss book bag along with the skullcap, pictures, and directions. While quickly dismantling the Glock 40 semi-automatic, He spoke to his partner as he maneuvered around in the front seat. "Make this quick right, right here." The overhead street sign read NW63Street.

"In a couple of blocks make this left onto Interstate 95 South to Exit 112W, then get in the left two lanes then merge onto NW 21 St. We not gonna pull into the airport, there should be a car waiting for us on 21st Street.." He rolled the window halfway down to toss the black latex gloves onto the express way. The bond these two had was inseparable. Brothers from different mothers.

"Red, you know I ain't tryna hear we driven back up top (New York City), right. We been in this truck to damn long today and I gotta piss as soon as we pull over. Up and down these highways all day looking for whoever that was you just hit." "Man, I really thought you was over that ish." Sul knew his partner was right, when he came home he was constantly going to the different prayers with his brothers, enjoying life until reality started to set in for him, when things just weren't going as he planned. "I know you're tired B, I am too. I also know you made sure I was good while I was gone and when I came home, but after this right here." He pointed down towards the bag between his legs. "Yo Wood, I got you in a minute. Trust me... Just trust me."

Sul half smiled at his boy then turned to look out the front window as he pulled out a dark gray, burnout cell phone, then put it to his ear.

"Yo, that's you in the black Lincoln town in front of us? Wood Flash the lights for me."

"Yeah that's us."

"Ok cool. Pulling up behind you now."

GUILTY OF SIN

1

3 **am New York City, NY.** Right outside of 1 Federal Plaza where joint F.B.I. Task Forces from several different states with top Drug Enforcement Agencies, along with the Bureau of Alcohol, Tobacco, Firearms and Explosives Brass stood side by side in front of the black on black Excursions gathered in what looked like a team football huddle before a game. The skies were turning from a dark bluish grey to overcast clouds as a light misty sprinkle had just started to drop. One of the agents standing towards the middle of the bunch was a slender built man, who looked to be in his mid to late fifties with sharp facial features and short chopped white hair, gold horn rimmed glasses and a clean shaven face, reached into the inside pocket of his black Burberry trench and pulled out a thick folded manila envelope and handed it to another well dressed, well-built man who looked to be the senior agent or agent in charge. As they quickly started to disperse to the unlocked vehicles, trading in their trench coats to obtain their windbreaker/rain flap style jackets embroidered with their respective government logos, pulled out a map displaying the entire island of Manhattan. All entrances and exits to the bridges and tunnels led in and out of the city. One section of the map was circled with a red magic marker and the lead agent out of the Eastern District of New York was now standing beside his comrade pointing

to a section of the map where his strike forces are to raid in just under a couple of hours.

"Listen gentlemen, these guys are very slick and without the assistance from our guy out of Atlanta, this day wouldn't be a blessing for most of us and I'm sure we all share the same feelings towards these men in one way or another. We can't mess this up and overpersue this. My guys tell me they should all be together by around 4:45am in their remote locations. Regardless of all the surveillance we've been putting together, please be clear that this may be the only time that we catch, or are gonna catch all these men together at one time. We have conducted simultaneous raids on all their houses as well. Simple! hit them and hit them fast, this way we can confiscate as much as possible before they can know what hit them.

"All these men are all considered armed and dangerous and I'm sure they will shoot if need be that's why I've taken so many precautions in assembling this team. We have snipers on roofs here, here and over here," as he pointed to the inside of the maps painted circle. "We also have a man on the inside who'll be driving them to their destination and alerting us once their private jet touches down in New Jersey. He will then call us a second time once all the occupants are in the penthouse. That's when well make our move, not even letting them get comfortable. This has to be swift because these guys now know that we're on to them. How? I don't know...It's like these men got someone undercover working in one of our agencies that's why all of you guys were hand-picked. Once again gentlemen, we will do this one strictly by the books. We'll be entering through both entrances, so prepare yourselves so that we don't come into cross fire once the flash grenades disperse. I'll lead the Alpha team in through the back maintenance entrance. You Agent Miles will lead the Bravo team through the front entrance and we'll have the whole block cleared to ensure us that no traffic will enter or exit this four block radius. He said as he once again pointed towards the circle of the map that he was holding in his hand. Once the host vehicle enters the perimeter and the first flash grenades go off, we don't need no new heroes. do u understand?" The tall, slender agent standing next to the lead agent folded the map, tucked it back in the manila envelope and placed it in his billfold. "Gentlemen," the FBI personnel who had just tucked the map. We will meet at the rendezvous point to take positions. I have a few men in place as I'm speaking to you just in case the occupant of the hosts house decides he has something else he has to do this morning.

"He's the one that's considered to be the most extremely dangers and he may or may not go down quietly. He's heartless and will have nothing to lose at this point so please be safe men." He then walked around the big, black Excursion truck and jumped into the back passenger seat as three other agents hopped in the truck as well.

The agent who shouted the first commands along with about ten other agents, walked back into the building of 1 Federal Plaza. The other agents proceeded to their vehicles to await their next commands. One more thing the lead agent said just before he pushed through the front door of the Plaza, NYPD's Commissioner, along with Mayor Bloomberg will be outside that building 2 hold a formal news conference once we ensure them that the security of the arrestees and perimeter is secured."

"vvvvvvvvv", "vvvvvvvvv", "vvvvvvvvv" "vvvvvvvvvwit". As Sheema walked out of their bedroom into the bathroom, she heard something vibrating in the next room and walked over to the table towards the sound of the vibration. "Bae, you left your phone in here and it's ringing."

"Can you pass me my phone before you go in the bathroom? I forgot I left it in there."

"Ok," she said looking at the number and as it started to vibrate again, she answered it for him. "Who is this?"

"Can you tell him it's a very important person from his past? Thanks." then became silent.

"He wouldn't even tell me who it is. You got some rude friends." She said as she walked back out then into the bathroom.

"Yo.. who is this?"

"It's ya other brother. And I know you know my voice." he paused as he tried to recognize and register that voice in his head

"It's me man.. ya boy.. Dam Sul I know it's been a min". Just as he was finishing this last statement, that memorable voice quickly came back into his memory.

"Oooooo shit. This can't be.."

"Damn man, I thought you forgot about me, my dude."

"Yooo, where they got you at now?"

"Nowhere bruh, I'm home and we really need to talk."

"When?"

"Now. What I mean is, how long would it take you to get to Teterboro Airport?"

"I don't know, about twenty minutes."

"Okay. Cool Bruh, I should be landing in about fifteen minutes. I was praying you'd answer your phone tonight."

"Aiight Beloved, see you in a few."

"Uh uh, where you think you going at this time of night, and who was that?" they real disrespectful."

" Bae.. be easy man.. you bug out over everything, you don't have to be a detective all the time."

" I'm not no dogone detective. It's almost midnight and some random guy calls. Doesn't want to tell me who he is, and now you're getting dressed too, I guess to go meet him. Am I right?"

"Yes you are Sweetie. You're one hundred percent right. Now you know I ain't just going outside in the middle of the night. Haven't done it since we been together. That was a very close friend of mine, more like a brother, when we was on the other side of the wall. He's from the South but he's only up here until tomorrow, that's why I told him I'll see him now." Rasul stood up and looked his wife directly in the eye, "you know dogone well I would never just leave out this house for nothing stupid.", he said With a seriousness she hasn't seen in a long time.

"Okay Bae. please be safe."

"I will," Now sitting back on the edge of the bed to put his wheat Timberland boots on.

"Imma call you in a few, okay." Grabbing his red Coogie sweater, and a red Philadelphia Philly's fitted baseball cap, he headed for the front door. She watched him walk out the room, then heard the door close. He pulled out of the driveway, and headed towards the private airport, all he could think was, "wow, it really worked" he wanted `to call his right hand man to meet him but thought twice about it. Then he wanted to call his cousin Esa, they knew each other from federal Prison, 'Naw, I ain't gonna do that either." His mind just kept racing about all kinds of stuff, and felt like a kid going to see his long lost brother, at the same time. Teterboro International Airport next right. He looked up at the sign then hit his right signal to turn onto the service road. A few seconds later, he hit his left signal to turn into the gate of the small airport.

2

Monday, February 14, 2002

"Boom! Boom! Boom!" came from the antique javelin of District Senior Judge, The Honorable Judge Billy "hang'em by the balls" Walls. His banged his javelin against his high desk as he raised his deep, raspy voice calling order to his court.

"Order in my damn courtroom. This bunch of shenanigans will not be tolerated from either side. Counsel, Defendants, and on lookers. I will band this whole courtroom's on-looking section." If I here as much as another loud whisper coming from that section. As he pointed towards the on lookers.

"Try me if you think that I'm playing any games."

"As for your defendants counselors," again he pointed his aging, bumpy knuckle looking index finger, this time at the entire defense table, looking over his gold horn rimmed glasses, from one person to the next.

"I'm sick of these scums of the earth coming through my courtroom, day in day out posing as if their sooo innocent, and especially them so religious Moslums ones. Shit, if you ask me, I think they're all terrorist, every god damn one of them, their high powered attorneys with fancy suits and million dollar life style from their ridiculously high priced law fees, but what they don't understand is I'm the top dog in this courtroom and I got the final say so here when it's all said and done If these damn hoodlums get found guilty at the end of these proceedings, I'm not just gonna throw the book at these guys I'm gonna flush the keys to their cells down the damn toilet as well." He said to himself as he shook his head while looking at the defendants as he turned away with a devilish smirk on his face looking directly into the eyes of the United States Attorney.

About a 100 feet to his left, out of the corner of his eye, he saw the steps of a small craft start to descend. "Vvvvvv, vvvvvvvvv, vvvvvvvvv" he looked down between seats in the cup holder at his phone vibrating. Quickly picking it up an flipping it open to see a now familiar number.

"Yoooo. what's good babe? You here?"

"Yeah I'm here. That you with them stairs coming down. You fancy, hun?"

"Mannnn stop trippen." "I'm coming down now. Where you at?.. Never mind I see you." The phone went dead as he watched his old friend slowly walk down those four steps then quickly over to the Silver Expedition, Sul hopped out the truck to greet and give his old prison buddy a big hug. "Damn Sul man, when you left Atlanta Penitentiary." They now stepped back a little from each other, but his boy kept speaking. "I would never had thought this day would come." "Damn, I really needed to see you as soon as I got out to thank you in person." This time with tears in his eyes he hugged his buddy again. "THANKS"

"What you did for me in Miami, words can't express the gratitude, I owe to you, my brother."

New York City, NY. Summer time in the wee hours of the morning on June 5th,1996.

"Bling, bling, bllingg, blinggg" she tapps her husband on the back of his shoulder to awaken him from a sound sleep. "Baby... Baby... Baby..." your cell phone has been ringing off the hook all night, almost every hour on the hour. Bae... it's almost 4am, who the hell is calling you at this time of the morning?? Baby, it better not be one of those whores from your cousin's club again acting like they're calling around looking for him to book a party or some other bull crap lie. I'm not playing with you boy!

"I haven't waited around all these years for you to come home, putting my life on hold to have to deal with these clown behind females, groupie chicks, I'm gonna leave your ass for real this time. Bae, I told you."

"Yo! Yoooo!, Sheema stop trippen and pass me the doggone phone. I can't believe this ish, neither one of us knows who's on the other end of that phone and your already convicting me. Breathe easy you bug out over everything, man." Sul said. I'm getting tired of this stupid phone" were his thoughts as his wife handed him his cell phone. "I thought I had that thing on vibrate anyway, man I hope this ain't none of those dumb behind females my wife talking about. Cuzzo know I'm tryna do the right thing wit wifey, because she's been a trooper." he said to himself for self- assurance as he pushed the phone closer to his ear looking into his wife's eyes.

"Yo who dis?" he said as he pressed the answer button on his phone with his thumb.

"Assalaamu Alaikum." (Peace and blessing be upon you). "Who the heck you think this is!!! Yo son."

" Walaikum As Salaam Family." he said, cutting his cousin off.

"Me and my father will be pulling up to your house in about twenty minutes aiight? We crossing the White Stone Bridge now, and he's talking about he needs his Dunkin Donuts coffee before we go anywhere, wow, and the sad part is he's dead serious.

"Yo… Hold up. Damn son, you sound like I just woke you up. I've been trying to call your house phone for almost two hours now. What, wifey got that ringer off again? That's why I'm blowing up your cell phone. Ak, I know you aint still in bed."

"Man Bae, that's crazy, why you turn the ringer off? I know you know you we have to be in Jersey before 5 o'clock this morning. We ain't leaving from Newark Airport, change of plans cuzzo I chartered us a flight out of the Clearport."

Get up mannn."

"Ahhh man, I'm trippen… I really forgot we supposed to leave this morning."

"Yo. Sul! get dressed, and give your wife our blessings." The phone went dead as he sat up, and slid off the bed all in one motion, then headed out of the room.

"Where you think you going at this time of morning?" his wife said as she now herself slid off from her side of the bed in tow to him. From the hall she heard the shower water bouncing off its walls and glass shower door.

"look. listen Bae... I told you last week, I had to take care of some business out of town with my cousin, remember? I've been running around with the kids at the center and we took them on a trip to a Knicks game tonight. I totally forgot what we had to do this morning."

" That's who that was on the phone?"

"Yeah... Him and my uncle are on their way here as we speak, so what I need for you to do for me real quick is put somethings in my carry-on bag for me, please.

They're gonna be madder than a mugg cause I don't got nothing ready yet. You know what... put the clothes you picked up from the cleaners yesterday in my bag. Oh, and those boots, and the Gucci sneakers and my Mauri's, there on the side of the pool table. Thanks bae at least I had a couple of my suits ready since last week there in my garment bag hanging in the hallway closet."

"Real talk Sul, I contemplated a long time before I reached out to you about my situation, I didn't want to drag you into my shit, or even worst, you back behind the wall with me." He raised his hand to stop Rasul from responding. "Hold up bruh.. I know a lot of people, but I've been gone for a minute, so I no longer really trust anyone, then I thought about some of the crazy ass stories you would tell me while we was working in that Prison factory, so I reached out to a good friend, who in turn reached out to you. By the time my man came to see me to let me know, what was good. Mannn.. you had already knocked dude off, I was like 'damn' and my man was like 'Yo. Ya man from uptop don't play no games, when I told him 75, he just told me to book him a flight for two to Tampa tomorrow, make sure it's a SUV ready to go, a burner, to full clips with a silencer and me there with the info for him.

When he's done I'm to fly him back on a non-commercial flight to an Air strip in Jersey, late that night because it should be done by then, In my head I was like who the FU@%, is this cat," Los got me dealing with. I just called your man Rasul and told him what you needed done and he was like, say no more meet me in Tampa with some cash, and have the rest ready when he calls, because that meant he was done. Yo then your dude Rasul calls me at almost midnight, and said it was done and they were flying out that night. Bring somebody to take the truck he used and get rid of it as soon as possible. I'm looking at the burnout, like who the hell this dude think he is, He must don't have a clue, who he's dealing with.

Anyway your man Rasul calls me again, we meet on the side of the road, they jump in the backseat as lowlow was getting out of the backseat, then jumped in their rental, so I brought them through the back of the Airport to my plane, he never asked me anything, they boarded, I handed him a bag with the rest of the money, that was it." "I told him you was funny with people you didn't know."

"You already know Los, I'd do it again for you if need be."

"I do know Sul, I had a new trial date and the dude you pushed was the lead witness on my case, without him they really had no case against me put I still kept pushing for a trial, so they offered me a deal. If I coped out to time served to keep the conviction, they'd cut me loose, so I was like bump it, I'm out, and here we stand."Carlos said as he extended is arms out beside him.

" Damn bruh, I'm glad your home, real talk, Los."

"Thanks Sul," they both hugged again. "I'm staying at the Holiday Inn in Teaneck. Do you know where that is?" I'm trippen because the pilot said it was only about 5/6 miles away."

"Yeah, that's about right. It's only about four minutes away from my house. I can take you if you want me to."

"Bet, this way we can talk. I got some real good news for you I think. What I mean is I'm not sure if your still on your Deen." he said looking at his home boy as Sul put his head down.

"Let's just say ... I still at least go to Jummah prayer on Friday. I fear Allah, but it's hard out here." "Get in the truck man." He watched with a smile, as his one-time jail buddy was really home. Rasul started the SUV and backed out heading towards the private airport entrance, making a quick right onto the service road. "What you gave me for your situation helped me out of a hole and I'm grateful for that." now making another right onto the interstate route 46 east, headed towards the hotel.

" That's why I'm here Sul, it's because I have a proposition for you. Just here me out, cool."

"Okay, cool."

"Do you remember what you told me you wanted to do if you ever got the chance?"

"Yeah.. I told you a lot of stuff Bruh."

"Nooooo Sul, imma just say this, if you had three hundred and sixty five days."

"O yeah I remember that. That was the only reason I said I'd hustle again."

"Ok.. now that I got your full attention, I'm here to take you up on that offer, if you think you can still make that happen." This time there was no quick response from the driver because his mind started racing a mile a minute. He knows he didn't hear what he thought he heard, there was about three more minutes of silence as they pulled into the hotels massive parking lot, but instead of pulling to the front so Carlos could check in, he pulled to the first available parking space.

"So you telling me you got someone that can make this happen for me?"

"No.. I'm telling you I'm gonna make this happen for you as soon as you feel like you're ready, if you still want it."

"Hell yeah, I still want the shot. I gotta make some phone calls and meet with some people, but hell yeah. "When? what I mean is, what kinda time frame do I have to get back to you?"

"Sul... You're the reason I'm home. You let me know. Ok? Now on another note, congratulations on the wedding, damn I wish I was home to be there. As a matter of fact... You busy in the morning."

"What time? Cause I gotta bring the kids to school in the morning, after that, I'm free for a couple of hours. Why? What's up, you want me to bring you back to the airport tomorrow?"

"Yeah, but I was gonna ask you did you know any of those car dealers we passed coming here."

"Yeah, I mean, there's one I dealt with all the time when I was getting money, called M & P Foreign cars. It's a little past the airport, but I'm sure they got what you looking for."

"Okay cool.. if you want we can grab some breakfast, then check out some cars. Cool."

"I ain't got no problem wit that." at this point his phone started vibrating, he picked it up and flipped it open to see that it was from his house. "Hold up Los. "Hello, hey bae."

"Hey, where you at? Are you ok?"

"I'm ok sweetie. I'm dropping my man off now, we still talking but imma be on my way in a few, okay."

"Okay, I'm going back to bed, see you when you get here."

"Iight, I'll see you in a few, love you."

"Love you too." the phone disconnected.

"Aiight Sul, imma let you get in the house, we'll talk in the morning." Los said as they shook hands and got out the truck. As He pulled up to the front of the hotel, got out and approached the service desk.

"Hello. I'm on my way, I'll be there in about fifteen minutes."

"Ok cool, imma be out front, when you get here."

"Aiight". About thirteen minutes later, Rasul pulled up to the front of the hotel just as Carlos threw what looked like a midsize duffle bag, over his shoulder, walked over to the SUV then jumped in. About an hour and a half later after a quick breakfast, they pulled into the foreign car dealership.

"Damn Sul, they got some shit here, wow, these cars are clean." Both now walking around the lot. "What you like bruh?" Carlos asked Rasul.

"Half the lot."

"Naw. Seriously if you had to pick something what would you pick?"

"I was always a Mercedes man, when I was hustling." he pointed to what looked like a new silver S600 AMG. "how much this?" he asked a short Hispanic male name Mauriceo, who'd just stepped out of the office, now approaching them and with whom his family dealt with in his past life.

"Oooooo shit, damn Ra, how you been?" it's been a minute since I saw you around these parts. How's your Pop's doing?"

"He good, stressful as always but all is well."

"What brings you around these parts, what you looking to get, I know you like this Benz."

"Yeah it's hot, but I ain't looking. My man looking to get something look out for him, he's fam."

"Whatever he wants." Mauricio the sales associate stuck out his hand, as Carols extended his as well. "What you looking to get?"

"Not sure yet, give us a minute, Sul, what else do you like besides the Mercedes?" Sul was already looking in the window of a 1995 red

Range Rover super charger 4.6 with black leather interior, then opens the front passenger door.

"I like this right here, cause you ain't gotta do anything to it." It already had tinted windows, and 20' black on black wide lip Asanti rims.

"I see.. I like it too, how I look in it?" Carlos said.

"In one word 'tuff', it's nice bruh.. get this.

"Aiight.. my man, lets talk numbers."

"Ra's my boy so imma do the best I can, let's go inside and talk numbers."

They followed Mauriceo back into the office. he sat at his desk and started punching numbers. "Y'all have a seat. I can let it go out the door for $69 grand, flat."

"What about the Silver S6, we were looking at to."

He turned back to the computer, started punching numbers again. "I can let that go, $85.5 if you really want it."

"Okay, for the sake of talk, Let's just say, I got $150 cash for both of them, could you make that happen." Carlos said as he looked from the car sales man then to his partner. "I'm about business, or can I speak with your boss."

"Naw, hold up, let me see something." The salesman said as he looked back at the computer then started punching numbers yet again, pulled a cell phone from his front pocket and started dialing a number in that phone, then put it to his ear, as he got up from his desk, then walked into a back office, with see through glass, and closed the door behind him. Three minutes later, he exited that small office headed back towards his desk and them. "If for the sake of just talk, you were serious, I could let it go at $150.5 best I could do." Carlos opened his duffle bag and grabbed to stacks of money. "Sul count this one, he tossed a thick wad of money to his main man, as he then started counting the second stack that he pulled out. "Sul gives him a hundred out of that." He counted what he told him to give, put it on the desk.

"Here Los."

"Naw, man hold on to that for a second. Here you go my man $150.5 like you ask for". Mauriceo started counting the money, putting the hundred dollar bills into ten thousand dollar stacks. He was at the fourteenth stack when he realized there was more money in his hands then he asked for. "Yo kid, this is more then what I told you." He said as he kept counting, "Yo this is a hundred and fifty five grand I told you 150, plus 5 hundred."

"I know what you told me I just wanted to see your honesty to my brother."

"This right here is what I do, I ain't no crud ball, Ra knows this."

"I'm sure he may, but I didn't, so now you should know, the rest is your commission for your honesty."

"Oh, shit good looking, damn Ra, you always had good family around you."

"Yo Sul, how long is it gonna take us to get to the airport." Now looking at his watch.

"five.. six minutes tops. Why what's good?"

"Man I told the pilot I'd be there before 12:30pm and its 12:15pm now."

"So what you gonna do?"

"Man.. we gotta go." Carlos said as he pushed back from the desk, then stood up.

"What..." Rasul said. looking in bewilderment as he and the salesman looked back and forth at each other, because his man had just purchased two vehicles, but now hoped up from the desk as his cell phone rang, looking at it, headed for the front door. Mauriceo had just put all the papers together for Carlos to sign.

"Not my problem buddy, Carlos said. You can take care of it once you drop me off."

"What do you mean? You want me to sign your name on them until you get back?"

"Naw.. I want you to sign yours, because their yours."

"Man, Los you play too much." Sul said as he watched Carlos walk out of the dealership heading in the direction of his Expedition. "Yo. Be right back let me see what's going on wit my peoples." Sul said to the car dealer as he now jumped up out of his seat, headed in the direction of his boy. 'Yo Los.. Los, hold up..' "What's good my dude?" Turning completely around to face his ex-prison buddy / brother.

"Bruh.. you've done more for me than you can imagine, this is just a small token of my appreciation Sul."

"Damn I don't even know what to say right now."

"Impossible, bruh you always got something to say."

"O yeah.. here." Sul extended his hand to Carlos to give him the wad of cash that he still held in his right hand. "Here man, it's the rest of your money that I didn't count while we was getting it together for dude."

"Naw Sul… that's yours too that's why I didn't ask for it back. I didn't realize the time we wasted this morning just reminiscing. Sul we gotta get there, time is money."

Rasul watched as his buddy jumped into the passenger side of the SUV. "Let's go Sul, gotta go."

"Aiight" he rushed around to the driver side.

"Yo.. yo, where ya'll going?"

"Be right back.. gotta drop him off". Rasul pointed east, while he was pulling off the slight curb. Now almost beside Mauriceo. "Gotta drop him off at Teterboro Airport, I'm right back in like 5,10 minutes tops to finish that paperwork."

Accelerating on the gas, as he now zoomed up the highway. "Yo Los you got me speechless right now, this money.. those cars, to which I don't even know what to tell my wife. Mann.."

"Sul listen, I'm home because of you.. So don't thank me yet, Thank me when you finish that, 365 day thing you talked about doing, I'm ready when you ready just give me a couple days in advance, and I'll set everything up for you." Carlos said as they was now pulling into the small International Airport.

"Man.. imma hit you in about a week. That's all I need."

"Okay that's cool, pull over their by that plane right there." as he was now pointing to the hanger marked 14. Los hopped out of the SUV just as quick as Rasul put the truck in park, now jumping out himself, then made his way towards the front of the small Craft. The dual hug say their farewell, Carlos boards as the pilot looks at him in a somewhat awkward stressed half smile. I guess it was because he was about a half hour late, and federal flight manifest, regulation requires, time is money.

3

"**9 11, may I help you.**" The police dispatcher said as the caller heaved heavily into the phone. "Listen, I don't know what's going on around here, but I just heard a couple of gun shots and some screaming. I, I, I think someone was just shot… what I mean is, I heard it. Then when I was about to leave my room, I heard someone running down the hall towards me so I ran back into the room. Locked the door then looked through the peephole. I saw a man who'd looked like he was bleeding. He had on a white T-shirt with a big stain that looked like blood by his shoulder area… But, wait a minute.. let me think… I think I also saw something shiny in his hand… I'm not sure if it was a gun or not." He said stumbling over his words trying to catch his breath at the same time.

"Clam down sir, please give me the address you're located at."

"I don't know the address, all I know is it's the Ramada Inn, in Fountain Heights on Highland and River. I'm on the third floor. I am directly across the hall from the room I watched the guy run into".

"What is the room number sir?"

"It's 3... 319 ma'am.. yes it's 319, please come quick... I'm not sure what's going on around here but this scene is becoming a little chaotic.

"Calm down sir.. I'll have a patrol car there shortly."

"Thank you, ma'am."

"Your welcome sir.. Sir if at all possible, please stay in your room until an officer arrives on the scene ok sir". As the dispatcher was talking the phone suddenly went dead on her as the called pushed the end button on his cellular phone.

Birmingham - Shuttles worth International Airport Summer of 1996 9:37am.

" Attention passengers the time is now 9:20am, the forecast at BSIA is 71 degrees with sunny skies, as we start our decent, we ask that you now take your seat fasten your seatbelts, and turn off your mobile devices, and as always thank you for flying American Airlines, have a great day". What looked like she was saying more to my brother, Big Melv, then the rest of the passengers on the plane. During our trip from New York in first class, we both noticed the stewardess showed my 6'5" 245lbs brother who would remind you of Ray Allen with a New York Yankees fitted and red and white Adidas sweat suit, who wear low ceaser hair cut with a full shadowed beard, pretty boy by my mother's grace, whom never had a problem with the ladies, She was a very pretty Haley Berry, but about 6'1" looking model as well, the only problem was, this was a business trip, and he played no games when it came to always being on point.

"Yo.. you see how she keeps looking at you bruh."

"Yeah, but I'm cool, if we see her on the way back I might holla at her."

"That might be about a week or two from now."

"Oh well. Yeah she pretty and all, but I don't need no distractions. Pops, or anybody else don't know I'm down here wit you and I wanna keep it like that."

"I feel you" looking out the window of the plane as it was now pulling up to the gate.

"364 days is all we need big bruh, but what I really need from you is to make sure my man's little brother is always by his self whenever you meet. At no time should anyone be with him feel me.. I would hate to have to do him dirty because he didn't listen, but our lives, wives and lively hoods depend on this." As they exit the plane Rasul was a half-step behind his brother walking through the door onto the gate's ramp when the head stewardess slipped what looked like a Mary kay business card into his hand, then looked up at me as I was now passing her with a big smile on her face, like I just caught her with her hands in the cookie jar.

"Have a great day sir."

" You to Lady."

"Yo.. before we take this ride how comfortable are you with this dude who gonna be moving all our money cause you don't even know him. I understand you and his brother was real tight, but we ain't got nothing on dude. How bout I bring somebody else down here that's expendable to us, so I can really keep a close eye on your man from the "A". I know y'all all Muslim, but shit, everybody got slick ways feel me. "Plus Pops don't know I'm down here anyway, I got a pretty lill young thang who works for the U.S. Customs that's gonna bring the money into his store. I'll always be at the drop as well".

"Work for Customs?" Man you nutts?"

"No just wanna be very smart and safe about this, feel me." "She grew up with us."

"I don't even wanna know."

"I'm cool with that." Big Melv said as they were existing the arrival entrance. "Yo where." Before he could finish what he was about to say, a middle aged Haitian guy, came from around a hunter green suburban right in front of them.

"Here, he's on the phone now." He said, as this random guy just passed Rasul his cell phone.

"Hello."

"What's up bruh? My man gonna drive you to Mobile Alabama. Sul I trust him with my life, so You already know."

"Oh okay cool, I'm like this dude looks real out of place, even up till he handed me his cell phone." "How far is it."

"About 4 in a half hours depending on the traffic, but at this time of day you should be good."

"Aiight cool guess, I'll see you in a few hours, beloved Peace."

"Peace Sul, can't wait to see you." They both disconnected as the driver put both their bags in the back of the truck, as they both jumped into the back seat of the SUV, then headed north onto 50th street, then made a quick right onto 18th Alley, with a couple more right turns to merge onto I-20W/I-59S, another left onto I-65S.towards Montgomery.

Almost 260 miles later the driver were began to make a left turn onto Dauphin Street, during that time Rasul and his brother were getting their master plan together, in short talks Sul also reminding his brother that Carlos doesn't know Big Melv was his brother. Now pulling into a driveway as Carols and another guy which looked like he'd came straight out of the jungles of Haiti. If my memory serves me correct I would have bet he was that guy name LowLow, that jumped into the rental that night we was at airport in Miami. A real rude boy. With his arms spread wide open. "Welcome to my world." Carlos said with a big smile on his face.

"Damn bruh it's always good to see you. Sul opens his arms as well to give his brother from another mother a huge hug. Los then looked over at the guy now exiting out of the SUV. He's also close to me like a brother just as we are." He pointed to Big Melv, his real D.N.A. brother.

"Shit if Sul sees you as his brother, than I see you as a brother as well, because I know for a fact this brother wouldn't have brought you all this way if he didn't trust you." Carlos extended his hand to Big Melv.

"What's up bro?"

"Chillin, Chillin, Skee." Melv extended his hand.

"Los." They said their names to each other as their grasps were releasing.

"Yo los damn man I gotta use the bathroom bad as hell".

"Down the hallway to your left." Without another word, Sul was up the drive way, heading down the hallway to the bathroom. "So how long you known Sul." He asked Rasul's older brother, Big Melv more out of just conversation than anything else.

"Most of our lives, we grew up on the same floor in our projects, he's more like a younger brother to me. He asked me to ride, so we here together feel me. I don't really ask to many questions because personally, the boy has always acted like he's before his time."

"Yeah I got that from him to while we were doing time together, he stays brain storming about everything."

"Yeah you right about that." Rasul's brother said, as Sul was now coming out the house."

"Yo Los. let's ride." Big bruh, you good? You aint gotta use the bathroom or nothing?"

"Naw I'm good."

"Oh okay. I need you to hop in upfront, I need to talk to my man in the back seat." Rasul said to his brother, as him and Carlos hopped into the back seats.

"Here's the keys, to both spots.. we got lucky there directly across the street from each other." He handed Sul two sets of keys and some paperwork. "This is the paperwork to both spots your now the proud owner of. They're in fake names." Carlos said as he went on, with the run down. "You may wanna change all the locks because their the same locks since I bought the houses. Just got the last one two days ago. This way you can have somebody always watching the other one, or whatever you choose to do."

"Aiight cool, I'll take care of the locks and stuff either later on tonight or early tomorrow morning. Two things. Where you staying Los?"

"Man, we just left it Sul, I stay real low to the ground in this town, no one knows when I'm coming or going feel me, we got a little land-scaping join that's actually doing well, even got a few Mexicans on the payroll." He said with a chuckle.

"How far is the pier?"

"That's where we going now.. it's about three to four minutes away" Carlos said as they were making a left off of Baltimore on to Gayle Street, looking at the Route 10 overpass.

"Listen Sul, the place we going to is on National Ave, a bunch of factories, your building is the closet to the water, it's the only other space they'll let us rent. It's guarded 24 hours a day. My guy is very good with faces. Now turning pass a guard booth, as the guard waves us by totally familiar with the SUV. Carlos pulls out what looks like a garage opener from the driver's seat back pocket hits a couple but-tons and door # 11 opens, then hands it to Rasul.

"All yours now buddy. Me and you are the only one with these. No one can get back here if they don't have one of these. It has a sensor in it that gets you pass the guard booth and twenty-four hour access, anyone else will have to stop at the gate, and trust me that's a big problem."

"Sounds good to me." Rasul tapps the front passenger, then hands him the remote opener. "hold on to this for me bruh". The driver now pulling into the building, where there were, two Newmans Medical Services vans, a big rig with a double sleeper tractor and two trailers, that read, "Nationwide Moving Company" on the side of the trailers. A forklift, what looked like medical supplies and a bunch of uniforms.

"Sul listen, whichever way you feel safe, you can either keep everything here, or do what you said. Personally, it coming here from Mexico, I speedboat my dope into Sarasota. and it's distributed from there. Just need a two or three day notice from you for your drop. Do you need a spot for your money?"

"Naw I'm good in that department, what's all this stuff in here for? Am I sharing this with someone else?" looking half bewildered.

"Hell no.. This is all you. Everything you should need to either move locally or anywhere you need to go." The paperwork, keys, and everything is over there, as they we're walking around the rig was a black on black Grand Cherokee. Before Rasul could ask. "Yeah Sul that's so you or whomever could run around with while you're here because it's even registered to the second house. There's even two social security cards, and birth certificates in the name of Ronald Robinson age 30, and Corey Hardcore age 27. If ya'll wanna use it or them to get a license. I also have access to as many more as you need, so depending on how many you need, just give me a day in advance to get them to you we got someone here at the Division of Motor Vehicle name Kat Davis, ask for her, give her the paperwork, and she'll do the rest, this way you don't look out of place if you get pulled over".

"Man say no more, you think she can duplicate multiple ID's in the same names?"

"Of course you no money makes the world go round, you just gotta slide her sum, But if she see you man." He looked back at Sul's brother. "She might want him."

They all laughed at that. "LowLow do me a favor, put all that paperwork and those keys in that bag on top of that tool box." The quite Haitian did as he was told, just as Rasul hopped up in the tractor.

"Big Bruh, what can you do with this."

"You already no." He said as Rasul hopped down and he climbed in. Rasul watched how his brother's face lit up, because of his passion for big trucks.

"Los, how much would this cost me when this is over?" Looking from Los to his brother back to Los.

"Sul, it's yours". He said with a sigh. All the money you about to see you ain't even gonna want this stuff when it's all over with".

"Naw, I think imma wanna keep this thing right here!"

"Could I see the keys to this thing". Big Melv asked looking at Los, while LowLow looked in the bag at the tagged keys, then tossed a key with a yellow tag on it up to into the window of the Rig. A half second later the giant truck came to life. He stepped on the gas two times as he looked down at his brother, with a big kool aid smile, then cut the engine and climbed down, then tossed the key's back to the Haitian as he was handing the bag to Carols. Then Los in a half turn hands the bag to Rasul.

"Ok now let's talk business."

"If you ready I'm ready." Lowlow do me a favor wait for us in the truck. Now looking at Rasul's brother.

"Ok so when?" Rasul said as he then looked at his brother, then back to Los. He good." I don't mind him hearing this, I know you trust your man who just got in the jeep, but that stopped here. Rasul pointed to the ground he was standing on. My bond with this dude, goes to the death of me." He looked Los directly In the Eye. "So what's the plan?" "I wouldn't be down here if I wasn't ready."

"You have a collect call from "Anass" an Inmate at the Atlanta Federal Penitentiary."

Press "1" if you except". Before Rasul let the whole message play out he pressed 1 to except the call.

"AsSalammau Alikum.." A opening greeting in Islam. " Peace be upon you."

"Walaikum AsSalaamu." Sul answered. Which is the universal greetings of "and to you be Peace."

"Alhamdu lillah." (Praise be to God) What's good my brother? I'm calling because I just received that money order and pics you sent me from South Beach. For a minute I thought you had forgotten about me or something. I ain't heard from you in over several months (God willing) all is well with you and the loved ones."

"They good.. All is well. Man I'd never forget about you just been caught up that's all."

"I understand.. Out of sight out of mind."

"Heck no. just trying to feed my family, feel me." You know the old saying it gets greater later. Well my brother, its getting ready to get greater."

"Word.. Man stop playing. I want outta here. I appreciate your help wit money thus far but I need some real money my lawyer want like 25 stacks (Thousand) on my 2255 direct appeal motion. He said I got great grounds to fight. Not tryna put a burden on your back, but you all I got for real, plus my lill brother."

"Ooh. How's he doing anyway?"

"He good." Before he could finish Rasul half cut him off.

"Yo.. remember that dream I told you about so many times when we was in that cell."

"Well lill bruh. My dude is home."

" Word Sul".

"Yeah. but hold up son. I met with him last week. As he was talking the operators voice came through the phone. Yo imma need you to get in touch with your brother so we can meet (God willing) ok ASAP."

"I got you Sul man.. thanks, I'm feeling like I may have some hope towards life on the outside, thanks Sul." Anass was still talking as the phone disconnected.

4

Thursday, June 5th, 1996 at 5:45am. Inside the windy city of Chicago's O'Hara International Airport, departure terminals luggage check in stands, and security check point.

"Junior, tell your mother I'll be home in a couple of days. She's acting like she mad at me, but I really got some business I need to take care of that will help us all out."

"Ok I'll tell her."

"Tell her I'll call her from our hotel room once I get there, got i!."

"Yeah I got you pops.. Yo you sure your flights gonna leave this morning with all this fog. It's been raining like crazy all night?"

"Siraj.. We up next, where your ticket at?" Siraj and his son turned a half circle to face the person talking. " It's right here." He said as he pulled his ticket out of his billfold, that was in the inside pocket of his new black on black Armani suit.

Siraj stood about 6'5" about 250 lbs. solid, built like the WWE Wrestler The Roc, very agile like a 150pound kick boxer, his ability as a Martial Arts Trainer and ex street fighter, deemed lethal if he had to use them. He always wore a freshly clean shaven head with a full beard of salt and pepper fur gave anyone who came into contact with him the impression he's not to be played with.

"Ashari... why you and my Pops look like ya'll going to a club or a funeral?"

"Naw, Junior. we aint go'en to a funeral, but we might hit a club or two while where away, you know..."

"Excuse me sir, I'm gonna need to see your tickets and your boarding passes."

Ashari, on the other hand was a large size man who stood about 6'2" 280 lbs. built like a defensive end for the Chicago Bears whom also practiced the arts and because he was a few shades darker than Siraj they nick named him shadow because he seemed to always be somewhere near Siraj at any given time.

"Excuse me Sir, I'm gonna need your tickets and boarding passes." The ticket clerk said once again as he turned from his nephew now facing her.

"Oh, excuse me too." Ashari said " My apologies pretty lady here you go." Extra smiles went back and forth from her to him clearly indicating both were interested in eachother, as she handed him the tickets back. Then she gives him, yet another seductive smile for a second time now. Her teeth were almost perfectly white as pearls with a Hallie Berry streaked hair cut which went well with her complexion about 6foot tall looking like Americas next top model instead of a ticket agent. Yeah... she wanted him.

"Hey sweetie... how are you doing this morning? But as for me I can't really say it's beautiful because it's been raining all morning, but I can say you made my morning a beautiful one with that smile of your face. Here". He now handed her their I.D.s InshaAllah maybe I can call you when you get off work, if you give me your number? Even better you can write it on the back of my ticket stub."

"First off what does "in shu lala mean?""

"No mah. He said with a slight chuckle it's In-sha-Allah which means "God willing" his fresh hair cut had him looking more like Gerald Levert headed for a Major stage show.

"I'm not sure if that's a good ideal." she said.

"Why not!" The clerk gave him a once over look then looked at his left hand, at a diamond incrusted platinum wedding band. " Oh this..." He now looked at his left hand as well. " I'm not asking you to marry me or anything, I'm just looking for a friend."

"Looks to me like you have a real nice friend, with that nice wedding band on."

"Listen." Ashari took another step closer to the clerk, placed his right and, palms up, on the counter to where no one could see in front of his massive shoulders.

"I'll explain, when I call you tonight ok. Long story and these people behind me." He looks back at the long line behind him then shifts so that she looks past him over his shoulders.

"They're getting a little restless." She wrote her name and number then told him to call after eleven o'clock tonight because she was off tomorrow." I'll call you tonight we talk then, maybe we could hookup in a few days when I get back in town." They both smiled at each other as she finished up processing their ticket information and luggage then passed him both stubs and their ID's as the trio now walked just a few steps towards the security check point. Junior shook his favorite uncles hand then hugged his old man. Then walked back in the direction from which they'd come in towards the departures entrance exits signs." Siraj, junior getting grow man."

"It seems like yesterday, when he was just a baby. Now look at him, he's almost 18 years old" was all Siraj could muster up out of that conversation as he watched his oldest son exit the airports entrance.

"Yeah I know… 365 days bra, 365 days…"

"You right!.. 365 days." Ashari answered back.

5

The police dispatcher, then dispatched to any available units, a possible shots fired, in the vicinity of, Highland and River, at the Ramada Inn.

"Dispatch this is car 107 I'm in that vicinity, I'm on my way only a few blocks away, over."

"Copy that 107.. I got a 911 stating possible shots fired, suspect or suspects may have occupied room, three, one, nine, from what the caller's description was the possible suspect ran into that room and may have been shot, plus he may have a firearm, so please proceed with caution car 107 over."

"Roger that!" dispatch I'm less than a block away and I can see from here that there's been some type of disturbance, I'm gonna need some back up... I have now pulled up to the Inn.. yeah looks like there may have been something going on." He said as he latched his mic back to the radio and looked at his partner. The patrol car pulled into the hotels parking lot headed in the direction of the main entrance.

There were a few people standing around in front of the Ramada, with looks of concern on their faces as the patrole car inched closer, one of the occupants at the hotel ran up to the driver's side of the police cruiser.

"We heard something that sounded like gunshots from near the pool area. So we ran towards the front of the building away from the shots; my children are scared to death look at them." She said with a very distorted look of concern on her face as she kept looking from the cop to her children.

"Calm down mamm… we'll take care of the situation from here." The drive of the patrol Car shifted from drive to park and opened his door to step out, now half in, half out of the vehicle he ached back into the car speaking into his mic once again.

"Dispatch… get me some," before he could finish his statement, two more cursers pulled into the hotel with their lights flashing every which way. Fast approaching they pulled to a quick stop, about 30 feet behind the first car, then exited their vehicles in fast military strides towards the already awaiting car that was at the scene.

"What's up Sarg." One of the men said as he neared his superior officer.

"You two… talk to these people and find out what you can and what they know, and may have possibly seen." "You three come with me." The other three policemen along the sergeant walked into the main entrance of the Ramada Inn, headed towards the reception's desk, but before they could reach the desk a tall lanky dark-skinned man wearing a burgundy blazer with the Hotels Logo over his name tag read "Corey White, Shift Supervisor," approached the four policemen in a quick manner. " Officers, I'm not sure what's going on". Shaking his head, back and forth.

" I as well heard what sounded like gunshots, firecrackers or something? I've been a supervisor here for almost four years and this is the first time I've heard anything like that around here before, I go to school right down… The lead officer held up his hand in a stop talking gesture. " You talk to this guy". He said and pointed to the lone officer to his left, then pivoted half left. " You two come with me". The lead officer who's a seasoned sergeant, that's been on the Fountain Heights Police Force for over twenty-four years, with only months left before his retirement knows he'll no longer have to deal with these catastrophic mean streets of Alabama to much longer. The sergeant

Stood about 6feet tall with a 190 lbs. who looked more like James Evens from that old T.V. show "Good Times." A well-respected Christian man known in the hood known as "Deac," which was short for Deacon of the Church whom always believed his job was to preach every time he had to arrest some petty criminal who may have had a chance in life. "Where's room 319"? The sarg. said, spinning back now facing the shift Supervisor. " Third floor, make two rights, it's at the end of the hallway near the vending machines". He pointed to a hand held map he pulled out of the inside of his blazer.

"Thanks'… lets go." The three officers headed for the elevator. They could hear the remaining patrolmen and the hotels super engaged in a short quick conversation just before the elevator door opened. They got off on the third floor, when dispatched notified the lead officer that more backup had just arrived and are entering the hotel as she spoke.

The triad rounded the second corner of the hotel's corridor towards room 319, when the sergeant noticed a couple, of suspected blood drops on the rug, and what looked like a slight smear of blood on 319s door knob. With the gloves he put on while riding the elevator he slightly touched the handle. "It's locked". He whispered to his partners, as one of his team crossed in front of him, then placed his ear to the door, as the third officer stayed behind the commanding officer. Just as the serdeant's patrol partner was about to move his head away from the door, he thought he'd not just heard a noise but a couple of voices over what sounded like running shower water and music from a radio or something...

6

BEEP, BEEP, BEEP, folled by three short beeps. " Man, I know that ain't them already?"

Sheema lifted one of the venetian blinds. " Yes it is." Esa is shaking his head as he is walking up the driveway, talking on his cell phone looking straight in my direction.

"Bae.. stall him out for a second. I'll be down stairs in a couple of minutes, I gotta put a couple things together…"

"Boy… you better hurry up!, Cause you know Esa be tripping, and it's too doggone early in the morning for his B-S…"

"Three minutes… that's all I need." Rasul told his wife.

"Ding dong.. Ding dong. "Here I come." She yelled from the top of the stairs does that boy ever sleep, every time I see him or talk to him, he always seems like he's wide awake. I can't see how Shameeka puts up with that. He's always on the go, especially since, his father and Uncle came home. "Ding dong." As the doorbell brought Sheema out of her trans, she hit the alarm key pad code number.

"Hey Sheem, what's up?.. Salaamu Alaikum…"

"Walaikum as Salaam.." Boy do you ever sleep?"

"Every time I'm home with my wife." He said with a little sarcasm. "Where's your husband at."

"He comin."

"How you been doing Sheem?" " Beep, Beep." Sul and his wife both looked in the direction of the horn, towards the end of the driveway. The window to the SUV came down.

"Salaamu walaikum, sweet heart."

"Hey Pops, My husband an Esa told me how happy they were that you were home too," that's great."

"Yeah, my wife told me to tell you to call her at work about 10am, I forgot what she told me I was half sleep when she was talking to me you know I'm getting old and senile."

"Pops, now you know you're not getting senile just maybe a little selective memory." They both chuckled. Yeah right you never sleep just like your nephew were her thoughts, "Ya'll be safe and please take care of my Husband."

"God willing I got'em Tesheem, talk to you later." Esa turned and started walking out towards the end of the driveway, just then, Rasul made his way through the front door, kissed his wife goodbye, with his bags in his hand, now half out of wind, from running down the stairs out of the house.

"Yo Sul.. Rasul, hold up cus." Esa said as Sul placed his Louis Vuitton duffle bags into the back of his truck.

"AsSalaamu Alaikum, son."

"Wa laikum Assalaam, Pops."As Rasul already had the back door opened to his 1996 Cherry red Range Rover 4.6 placing Esa's luggage on top of what was already there. The two then started to jump into the SUV, headed for one of northern Jersey's private international air strips, and their new fate that would lie ahead. Until reality snapped him back into that moment.

"Help me with these bags." Sul turned around and with a quick two step grab his father's bags. Outta Esa trunk " Yo Sul! This should be a good trip. I need this." He stated as he'd made direct eye contact with his big cousin. Esa who was about 5'8", with a well-built 175 lbs. frame gave off an impression of a Westley Snipes type, just as fast, and he was into conditioning his mind, and body. His every day was to seek the pleasures of his Lord, his only problem was all he needed was just a little more to get him over the hump, so he can really devote his time to the children he's been dealing with down at the Islamic Center. Esa's wife had been the bread winner even since his release she's held things down even though he was currently working as well, but his ends was just enough to get by. If this works out. "Allah I promise I'll never do anything else that will displease you. But right now I need help. I know it's wrong and I'm sure you'll deal with me because of this but I gotta do what I gotta do." were his thoughts as he jumped into the truck his thoughts kept rolling. It was only lights years ago when he and his cousin would play as kids, until they went their separate ways during their high school years. Esa was a very smart student and a profound artist, voted most likely to succeed, in the business world, by his junior year. Rasul on the other hand was also what you would call a thinker n very smart, but a sports joc, with dreams of becoming a pro football player one day, as he stayed in the local newspapers. He stood about 6'1", 275 lbs. light skinned chinky eyed low waive hair cut with as many tattoos as any subway in Harlem, NY. not always flashy, but very cocky also built like a football player, passive aggressive that played in the streets hard one of the deadliest of Shabazz's children, whom always thought big and looked at the bigger picture instead of the right now. With high hopes n aspirations at every twist and turn. Disaster struck in the winter of 1985, when Esa, his father Hakeem, and his Uncle Shabazz, who was already doing time for tax evasion. two of Sul's brothers were indicted by the government, on multiple conspiracy charges to distribution of narcotics trafficking. Esa his father, and two Sul brothers received ten years, while Rasuls Father was sentenced to an additional ten years on top of the eleven, he was finishing up, for being the so-called mastermind from behind the wall. This was a global plea that everyone had to take or trial would mean a minimum of thirty years a piece plus. It's said that lighting doesn't strike the same place twice. Well.. Disaster struck again only four years later, when the Government came knocking once again, trying to hammer Sul's father Shabazz and Uncle Hakeem on some money laundering charges. Rasul couldn't see them being punished to anymore time, so he took and chose family loyalty over his childhood dreams, and turned himself in for six hundred and fifteen thousand dollars, that was found on yet another one of those drug sweeps aimed at Shabazz's nightclubs, he purchased in Harlem, back in the late 70's. One of Shabazz's street Capo's, who couldn't bear the thought of losing his girlfriend for a few years decided to work for the government. When Sul turned himself in for the money and provided the paperwork, showing the club had been in his name for some years now. The government took a blow, because up until this point Rasul had never been in any real trouble. So the United States Attorney's office snatched the deal back from his father's Capo. Then turned around and sentenced him to twenty years for lying to them about the club. Sul's mother couldn't understand, why her son would throw his life and dreams away for his already convicted father, who just couldn't let go of the streets.

7

"Inmate Anas Shakir cell 528.. you have a visit." A guard shouted in the direction of the top tiers day room, twenty seconds later a caramel complexion freshly shaven head, broad shouldered man totally drenched in sweaty prison issued ka-kis and what looked like an old wife beater (tank top) that Freddie Kroger shredded in his first night mare on elm street movie, with a pair of inner rubber work gloves on his hands.

"Who he just called?" he said to no one in particular but out loud anyway."

"You.." The guard said as he started to walk back towards the stair case leading towards that particular day.

"Oh.okay, I'll be ready in five   minutes aight?"

"That's all you got is five more minutes buddy, because we gonna lock down for the 10 am. Count. He said as he looked at his watch then looked up at Anas as he took off to grab his shower stuff for a two minute rinse off. In November of 1989 Rasul was sentenced to seven years in Federal prison. The passenger side of the SUV's window slid down once again.

ॐ

"What cha wanna do sarg?.... Want me to knock!"

"No. No... Don't knock, we want to surprise who's ever in there."

The sergeants partner slowly backed away from the door, Then reached in this back right pocket, and pulled out his black combat shooting gloves. With a little more excitement than he should have had. "Ding". The charm from the elevator indicated the door just opened, then the sound of the police radios could be heard as the officers were fast approaching. They rounded the corridor, where the triad stood. The lead officer then signaled to the three other officers, to turn their radios down, by putting his right index finger to his lips in a whisper gesture, making a "Shhh" sound. Neither officer knew, but from almost 25 years of experience on the police force. A surprise attack always left the opposition with the upper hand. More whispered tones came from the room. "there may be gunman in there."

8

R aleigh North Carolina. 1am eastern standard time. June 5th, 1996.

"Hurry up.. We were supposed to had been on the road by midnight, we already late damn! An hour behind schedule, when I give my word at something, it's as good as a sealed deal."

"Daddy, I'm sorry... I just wasn't sure what I wanted to wear down there, and you know I have to always look good for you." Betty was the Pamela Grier of the new millennium every time she left the house she had to look good. Originally from Queens New York, she was always a sight to see whenever she hit the streets. In her younger years, her dreams were to work in telecommunications as a talk show host.

She fell in love with Hakeem at first sight. Before him she had never seen as much money as he had in her life and as a matter of fact she didn't think black people walked around with that type of money if not for sports. It turned her out, she left her job at a local television news station to become a full time Bonnie to her husband Clyde, He and she stood the same height at 5'7", they became inseparable in many ways, she was always down for him in whatever he did, and he of course knew this as well.

"Yeah.. whatever. because of you my family is gonna look at me crazy. You know how my nephew gets. By the way did he call again?"

"No he didn't, but your brother did… He said their flight should be landing around ten minutes to seven, this morning."

"Damn girl, get your ass in this truck and drive… Why the hell didn't you give me the phone when he called."

"I told him that you were on your way back from the bar. You went to let Tom know you'll be out of town for a few days, bae you left your cell phone at home at the time, so I couldn't call you know you no, I know not to talk on land line phones."

"Damn, lets ride." Hakeem said as he buckled into his seatbelt of his silver ML 420 Mercedes truck as she backed up out of their drive way, onto the main road with her foot pressed to the floor on the gas pedal. They only lived a minute away from the interstate on 6forks rd. it only took them 4 minutes the way she was driving before she pulled onto I-40W headed 85 south bound. Hakeem looked over at the gas gauge and noticed, that the tank was only half full.

"Betty.. I thought you said you put gas in here!"

"I did put gas in here last night!"

"Girl when I called you from the bar not even twenty minutes ago, I specifically asked you did you put gas in the friggen tank! Look at the damn gauge."

"Well damn you too! I thought it was still full. Hakeem ever since you came home from prison this time you've been talking to me like I'm a piece of shit. I ain't the one who shot you and I sure as hell ain't the one who put your ass in that wheelchair. The police did that shit… I've been the only one by your side all this time though thick and thin, hell or hot water I been that bitch by your side. All I've ever done up till this point was try.. try to make you happy.. try to help you erase your pain and I even helped you find your son! so cut me a damn break, shit!"

"Sorry baby, I'm apologizing Betty.. It's just that I've been going through a lot since I've become confined to this wheelchair." While he was finishing up his sentence the cell phone started to ring. The Starteck Motorola indicated his Nephew number was calling.

"Hold up Baby.. please hold that thought." They pulled into the next service station they saw. " Ok bae." She said as they looked at each other like they knew what each other was thinking, because for so many years they've done this same exact thing with each other, and shared lots of memories and memorable moments.

"Asalaamu Alaikum, Nephew."

"Wa laikum as Salaam, little brother."

"What's the happs big bra? I thought you were your son."

"Naw.. He told me to call you back, to make sure all is well and to make sure everything was going as planned."

"Yeah well, I'm about an hour behind schedule, but Betty said she was gonna make up some time on the expressway you know she's a speed demon."

"Breathe easy little brother and be careful remember safety is always first! If you're not at the airport by the time our plane lands, we'll call you to see where you're at. If you're not close enough when

we depart the plane we'll just have to meet you at the hotel, ok...
Please give your wife the Salaams."

"Yo! Shabazz.. luv you big bra."

"Yes, I know this just drive safe. This meeting is very important to
all of us. My son is determined about this one. He's held us down for
years while we were behind those walls. We can't let him down, you
digg."

"You've made something special out of that boy, even though we
messed his football dreams up!"

"Now on that note little brother... Salaamu Alaikum good
brother."

"Walaikum as Salaam." Shabazz pushed the end button as fast
as he could looking over at his son then looking down at his freshly
manicured nails thinking about how he wrecked his son's life and
how he's gonna try to make good with this situation.

Hakeem closed the flap to his phone, then placed it in the trucks
console, thinking of how that boy could have probably made it to the
N.F.L., but because of the loyalty to this family he chose to take some
prison time to keep us from still being confined. We really need to
act on whatever he wants to talk to us about and make it work.

"Count time, count time, it is now 9:50 am all inmates are to report
to their cells for the 10am count. Count time, count time." The cell
block officer yelled walking from one end of the unit to the other.

"I'm ready." Anas said half out of breath and half dressed as he ran up to the officers station to get his visiting pass to leave the unit.

"Another minute an your visit would have been waiting until after this count cleared, and you know you ain't had a visit in about six months he was saying to his self as he started to leave the unit headed down the stair still fixing his clothes that were freshly pressed since yesterday when he'd gotta a letter stating that he'll be getting a visit today that needs to take place because it may be the most important visit of his life."

"Hakeem... Hakeem!"

"Yeah betty what's wrong.."

"You were so caught up in your thoughts... Give me the money to pay for the gas."

He grabbed his little Gucci tote bag from under the passenger seat, unzipped it, then pulled out two brand new fifty dollar bills.

"Here get me some coffee please.. It's gonna be a long ride." He handed her the money then grabbed her by her arm firm but gentle. " Baby... no matter what.. know that I'll always love you!"

"What's wrong bae?"

"Nothing.. Sometimes I get beside myself that's all. Give me some sugar." They kissed like it was twenty years ago very long and passionate.

9

"**M**r. Assistant United States Attorney, do you have any more questions for the witness."

"No your Honor.. I don't."

"Do you have any more witnesses at this time, before we start the closing arguments."

"No your Honor, the prosecution rests for now." Just as he was finishing that statement. From behind Assistant United States Attorney, a tall clean cut white man whom looked a lot like Bruce Willes from those diehard movies wearing a long-sleeved white button up dress shirt with a blue wool vest grabbed the shoulder of the assistant attorney as he was about to be seated. He had just walked into the courtroom not even two minutes ago, whispered fast tones into his ear before he seated himself behind the attorney. In another full swing motion with one hand raised in a stop gesture towards the judge. "Excuse me your Honor, we just found out we may have a problem with one of the witnesses. Your Honor, if need be, the government may need to bring this witness back. The government would greatly appreciate if your Honor could order some type of immediate protection for our star witness as well."

"Please thank you counsel, I will put in an order of protection for now, then have the U.S. Marshalls office get me all the proper paperwork together before the end of court proceedings today. The Judge then look towards the witness stand at the Star witness.

"You may step down, please follow those marshalls that are standing over there." He pointed towards the far end of the courtroom.

"Okay," he said as he stepped from the witness stand, then walked down the aisle towards the back, were all eyes in the courtroom followed the witness as he headed in the direction of the awaiting armed Marshalls.

"Counsel are you ready?" he said as to no specific defense Attorney, but at the table itself.

"Yes your Honor we are." As the lead counsel of the Black Brothers Of Promise; (B.B.O.P.) organization rose from his chair, adjusted his tie, then placed his pen on the top of his note pad. Counsel stood almost 6 foot 4' built like a lifelong marathon runner with his deep Miami skin tan and his almost white salt and pepper hair slicked back in a ponytail, the black on black Hugo Boss two piece custom fitted sports suit with his wood grain and gold horn rimmed framed Cartier glasses and gold cuff links set off the black, gold, and white tie he had just purchased from Neman Marcus the night before. This big shot shark of organized crime cases was well renowned throughout the country for his no holds barred Paraná tactics sucked in yet another deep breath of this two month long trial that's now coming to who has the best sounding story to the jury. He who hasn't lot a trial in almost four years, brushed off some imaginary lint on his tailored jacket pockets, then headed in the direction of the witness stand, but stopped just short of the stand. Put both his hands on its guardrail section of the jury, just short of juror number 3. She was wearing a white sun hat, and a red and white sun dress with a bow at the cleavage of her chest.

$$\sim$$

Parkside Village, Fayetteville Georgia: Just before 7am, June 5th same year (1996). I know I should have drove up here last night. I don't know why Heed wants me to come up anyway, If he don't trust those New York cats, he shouldn't mess with'em... Now he playing games, I just talked to him on the phone not even ten minutes ago.

"Yo. Who dis?"

"It's me man! I'm almost at your house, what time we gotta meet those dudes?"

"My brother told me to meet them at the Lenox Mall at eight this morning sharp Anas said, maineman is never late for anything."

"Aiight, I'll be at your house in five minutes. I just got off of the interstate."

"Yo. Man, Im gonna open the door now, so you don't have to ring the doorbell, but yo! Don't make too much noise I think my girl still sleep. Man I don't need her coming down stairs asking no questions being noise you heard!" I'm in the basement cleaning my heat."

"I'll be there in a minute." Hamid hit the end button on his cell phone. Turned his radio back up and twisted the rim of his fitted hat to the back as he turned the corner onto his cousins block, passed a few houses as he pulled into Heeds two car driveway.

"Damn man, I just told his ass not to make no noise when he gets here now his stupid butt got that damn music blasting early in the dag on morning." Tauheed stepped out onto his front porch, as Gena was already halfway down the stairs.

"Boy... Where you going?"

"I gotta take care of something for Anas baby. He wants me to meet somebody for him, remember the note you gave me from him when you went to see him. Well.. let's just say I'll be home in a few hours ok?"

"Okay. Now. Who in the hell is that blasting that damn music like he's crazy?"

She said as she brush between her man and the front door trying to see just who it was.

"Bae, I already told Hamid to turn it down. I'll call you at work when I get back okay G.. Love you." They kissed as she goes back in the house and Tauheed closed the door behind him, His cousin was already making a U-turn in his driveway.

"Come on Heed, let's ride! You drive." He shouted thru the open window, of his black 1995 B.M.W. 528i, as he shifted into park, then jumped across to the passenger's side seat, before his could even respond and answer him, Heed jumped into the driver's seat, pulled out of his drive way, headed in the direction of interstate 85 north. "Yo! Where that ish at cousin light it up Bro." Hamid said to Heed as he dug into his own pocket and handed the driver an already rolled blunt.

"Yo! Heed, why Nass wants you to meet those cat's so bad?"

"When Geina went to see him two weeks ago for me," he passed her this note as she was getting ready to leave while he hugged her, when the visit was almost over. He passed his cousin that same note;

Yo Ty,

Assalaamu Alaikum, Peace and blessing beloved, I got some real money headed your way plus it will help me pay for all my legal fees. You gotta meet with my old cellie, his name is Rasul. These dudes are major players out of New York and New Jersey. He told me he was gonna lookout for me, and take care of my lill'bra on the streets as well. You'll be dealing with him, but don't worry it won't be for long. Ty' he's a real dude, please keep it 100 with him, because he's also a "certified Nutt". We'll talk about that another day and time. Meet him at 8:30am in the front of the Lenox Mall. Peachtree entrance, right across from the Swisstell Hotel. He's seen pictures of you, so he knows who you are, and what you look like. I know you've led your own team and did your own thang but lill'bra, best trust me on this one, we all need this!

One love, ASA

Anass

"Yo! Heed… His cousin said as he passed him the note back, Heed hits the cigarette lighter. It pops out and he places a corner of the note into the red light, the note started to smoke, then lit on fire. When the paper was almost burned he rolled down the window and let the small piece of paper life in the wind. "you may need to bring me in on this yo!"

"Listen it ain't like I don't already get money, I don't even know this cat Hamid.

Let me talk to him first. If I'm not feeling that dude, I'm out. "Nass just gonna have to understand." "Feel me."

I ain't sure what Anass told this cat, but I ain't never really been a hustler. I hit banks and people who really got it, I don't know what big bra's dude wants from me but, I ain't hustling for nobody it's that simple."

"That's what I'm talking about by you letting me in. If this cat from up top got work, let me move it! We split it, know what I'm say'en."

"Yeah I hear you cus, but I don't know... Let's see how this plays out !""

"You got that." Hamid said as he turned 2pac's new cd back up and thought for a second then. " Yo! Heed.." He he turned the radio back down. " When I was in Leavenworth U.S.P. I was cool with this brother name Esa. Rumor had it on the compound, that he and his family was getting a lot of money up top. He should be home now too. If I get a chance to talk to them dudes you're getting ready to meet, I'm gonna ask them do they know him."

"Hamid, New York is big as hell..."

"They still might know him.. If they don't, so be it!"

"Listen Hamid.. Why do you keep saying they. It's a him, not a they."

"Now you listen cousin… those cats from up top don't move alone I was locked up with a lot of those dudes trust me."

"Hamid.. Fall back and let me talk to this dude and at least fill him out… You already making plans and we ain't even seen this dude yet, so breathe easy and pass that ishh." He passes the blunt and continues to talk.

"Sorry cus.. It's just that note Anas sent you really got me wanting to meet this cat Rasul, or whoever he is…"

10

In more whispered tones, this time it was from the officers.

"I think we should act fast before they realize that where out here some place, or on the other side of this door."

"I'll hit the door sarg, Ok?"

"Ok I'll cover you, you four.. He pointed with four fingers to the men standing to his right, cover us and bring up the rear as we enter, remember stay close and alert, we can't let this get out of control." Sargs, partner rammed shoulder first into the door with the commanding officer, right on his heels. As the door exploded open, to triple X action going on in the double bedded room at the far end of the wall, between what looked like a young a young woman and a older male. The sex dual stopped in mid stride as the door to room 319 blew open. They looked over at the uniformed men who were now filling the room. The man who was just knee deep thrusting his way into an exotic ecstasy of paradise, dove off the woman, in another motion to the opposite side of the bed, as the female laid stunned, then slowly slid the covers up over here body, as the men inched closer to the dynamic sex dual.

"Don't move another muscle on the other side of that bed, or your ass is dead meat!"

"Do you understand me sir."

"I'm not moving anything officer, I was just going for my pants."

"Don't move.. don't you move a muscle!"

"I'm not.. I'm not moving anywhere." As the man was finishing up his statement.

The sergeant thought he recognized that the voice on the other side of the bed, where the naked man had dove too. What he saw quickly clouded his current thoughts and almost brought tears to the eyes of this seasoned twenty-four year officer who thought he'd seen just about everything.

Atlanta Georgia, June 5th

"Hello this is the Swisstell Hotel." Before the recording could playout, Rasul hung up his phone for yet the third time.

"Damn man.. Why the hell ain't these people answering the phone?" "Yo Esa.. do me a favor.." He handed his phone to his cousin. "Keep trying the hotel number for me because I need them conformations before everybody gets there, ok."

"You got it and I'm on it."

"I already left a couple messages on Sirajs cell phone, his plane must not have landed just yet, I told him to meet us at the hotel if he doesn't see us when his plane lands." As he hands Esa his phone cell phone.

"Yo! Sul." He pushed the cell back up front. " here you go. Somebody just picked up the hotels phone."

"Aint that about a bitch." "Hello… how you doing today?, yes.. I'm just trying to confirm my reservations.. yes.. Rasul Young.. yes.. eight rooms.. ok yes.. 19th floor..C to J.. yes.. I'll be there shortly." Sul hung the phone with the receptionist, as Sirag was calling. He then tapps his father as he pushed the send button answer it.

"Yo! Pops Siraj is calling me now."

"Well answer the darn thing."

" I am Assalaamu Alaikum, Beloved."

"Walakum as Salaam, lill bra, I just got your messages." Sul stopped him in mid- sentence.

"Cool.. When you get to the hotel, hold up." He reached over and lifted the console under his right arm for the napkin he was just writing on from when he was talking to the hotel operator. "Here's, the comp number.. they should give you all the room keys.. There all on the 19th floor, and separate keys I'll get them from you when I get there aiight?"

"Okay big timer.. I see your work."

"Naw, man.. don't do that… Just know a few people that's all."

"Whatever you say, I'm here and where ready... I'll see you when we get there."

"Cool.. Siraj listen. I gotta meet Anas's little brother and get a feel of him first, before he can meet everybody, if I get a bad vibe I'll give him a couple dollars for Anas and send him on his way you dig.. but if he's anything like his brother says, then we good. "Feel Me."

"Sul, this is your ship, I'm just on the boat."

"Naw, big bra.. This is our ship, and we gonna own the boat when it's all said and done, because when this is all over we'll be set for life God willing real talk."

"I hear you."

"Alhamdu lillah (All praise be to God) you hear me, but I need you to feel me on this one as well. Aiight bro I'll see you when I get there, Salaams."

"Peace," both phones when dead. This wasn't Rasul's first trip to the A.T.L. nor was it his first stay at the Swisstell. The Hotel was like his second home any time he'd come to Atlanta he always stayed there. The trio walked into the Hertz car rental office. Sul pulled out his wallet and with to forms of Identification and his now black card, he rented a 1996 dark green 4 door Yukon XL to make their movements around the city in comfort. Rasul tossed the keys to Esa just after he signed all the agreements and paperwork, they handed him back his ID and credit card, as he and his cousin picked up their luggage. Shabazz didn't have as many bags as the other to so he decided to grab his sons book bag.

"Sul, what the heck is in this bag.. It feels like a bunch of books or something, 'What' you going to the library or something?" his father said with a slight s mirk on his face.

"Naw, it's some important paperwork, that's all." They walked down the ramp to where the SUV sat parked, as his father Shabazz dropped his bags in front of the back barn doors, of the 4x4, then walked to the driver's side back passenger door, opened it then hopped in, and didn't even look back at the bags, as his young ones loaded the luggage, then made their was swiftly out of the crowded airport, and thru college Park, headed for the Metro area's main Mall. Now Shabazz's cell phone started ringing.

"Hello and Salaamu Alaikum little brother.. Where you at?.."

"We just passed a sign that said Atlanta Downtown and Peachtree Street. Lenox Mall next exit, but where headed towards the airport to me you!"

"No, No.. Where on our way to the hotel as we speak so take that exit, we picked up a little vehicle for our stay.. We'll meet you at.. "What's the name of that place you know I'm getting old?"

"The Swisstell pop's" his son answered.

"Yeah meet us in the front of the Swissteller or whatever it's called. We'll be there shortly."

"Ok big brother, than I guess we'll meet you there."

Shabazz pushed the off button to his cell phone, as they drove north on the Interstate, out of the corner of his eye he watch as his sons eyes where straight ahead but his mind was a million miles away. As all Sul could think about was him one day making this dream a reality ever since he'd been released from federal prison, because the only rehabilitation he got was how to flip, cut, and turned cocaine better, faster and get a bigger pay day. He also became very good at reading peoples body language. His temper was always short fused because of gunshot wounds he sustained which ended his football dreams. By the time his cousin Esa came home he was moving at almost a 7/8 kilos every two weeks thru the help of his boy Hollywood on one side of town and brothers little Cee and Hardcore Gambino in the Sugar Hill Housing Projects on the other side of town. His excuse to himself was as long as he wasn't touching it he wasn't selling it, but truth be told ever since he took that trip to Miami to help his man out things ain't never been the same since in his life, no more praying, hanging out a little more at night, and the Friday Jummah Prayer is almost nonexistent. Now that his family was all home it was time to put his biggest plan into action, once and for all...

11

They made a left turn down Lenox off of Peachtree. The Swisstell sat on the right hand side while the Lenox Mall was on the left.

"Esa." Rasul pointed to his far left. "See that black B.M.W. parked by the malls entrance it's out of place. That must be Anas lill'bro pull past him slow, then turn around so that my side of the truck can be on the B.M.W.'s drivers side ok... just in case it's not him, got me."

"You got dat!" Since Esa's release from federal prison all he lived and breathed was Al-Islam, but knew this trip was out of pocket to what he himself was teaching those kids back at the center, at the same time, bills just kept pouring in as Shameeka kept complaining they needed help. Most of his days would be either at the Masjid or helping the youth in his community. Doing community service mostly. That wasn't paying the bills and the little night job he had with the cable company had him living from check to check. He knew the whispers of the devil were everywhere and doing the right thing would keep him out of jail. It would keep him a free man.

BUTT!

"But all this is gonna take is 365 days and I'll be set for life." These were the thoughts as he turned down the radio as his cousin Rasul lowered the passenger's side window.

"Yo son.. Yo.. You Tauheed?" He responded as the bmw's window slowly came down.

"Yeah.. Yeah dat be me." Rasul opened the trucks door, then got out of the vehicle.

"Yo Son, lets walk and talk!" Tauheed fixed his Atlanta Braves fitted hat, then turned it to the front of his face, then hopped out the car, then walked away from both vehicles towards the valet parking area entrance.

"Yo, your brother was my cellie for a few years I'm sure you know this, as I grew to love him like a real brother. He's told me a lot of good things about you." Sul said with a sly smirk on his face. "Your ability to make money disappear to off shore accounts, which may come as a great gain and asset things of that nature. I gave Anas my word, I would set him straight. Like I'm telling you now. I love him as if he is my real brother, and because he's yours, I now love you, as a real brother. I ain't down here to find workers or play any games… I'm down here to gain partners, you dig…"

As Rasul was talking, Tauheed was starting to like this cat already, he wasn't sure why he was just having that good feeling this dude was telling him the absolute God honest truth. "I'm now gonna introduce you to our fam in the truck, then the rest of your family at the Swisstell". As they walked he went on. "I copped a room for you at the hotel as well, it's paid for, for a week, I'm not sure where you live, but it's yours to do what you do, "you digg me." With a smile Tauheed extended his hand as Rasul's hand had been already stretched out. When their hands clasped, Rasul pulled his new found family member into a bear hug. Then he whispered into his ear as if they were in a loud crowded room. " When I tell someone I love them. Believe it! When I tell you don't trust it. Believe it! When you hear me say he and or she, gotta go."

"Death is my only option believe it!!! They mutually broke the embrace, then headed near the SUV. Rasul waved the two occupants out of the truck. "Yo, this is Anas's lill'bra Tauheed. Ty this is my father Shabazz and my cousin Esa, who's also my right hand man." But before Heed could respond back, his thoughts started rolling fast.

"Holy shit.. My cousin was just talking about these cats." Only Hamid couldn't see the because they were parked on the opposite side of the car's passenger side facing the opposite direction. They were about to all exchanged handshakes, as Tauheed said the Islamic greetings of Peace. "Assalaamu Alaikum."

"Walakum as Salaam," was almost said in unison, as Shabazz quickly said.

"I smell marijuana," then chuckled. Tauheed clearly had a look of embarrassment not because he had just smoked but because he had just greeted them high. Changing the subject just as fast Heed said as he looked at the shortest person from the up top crew.

"Esa.. That's your name." Ty said with a smile.

"Yeah, why what's up?" he said with a how do you no my name look on his face.

"Naw.. Naw.. It's funny right. I got a cousin name Hamid, who's from Alabama, who used to talk about a cat from New York, he was in Leavenworth USP with, and his name was Esa, the same as yours."

"What's your cousins last name?"

"Baxtor". Tauheed rolled his name off the tip of his tongue.

"Yeah, I know him, I'm the one who gave him that Attribute. Unk you remember my old cellie Macky Baxter from Alabama right... Thought he was a pretty boy loved to take pictures." Shabazz smiled to the memories as he fixed his glasses on his noise.

"Yes, I remember.. he was a very good brother. How is he anyway?"

"Shit! He's in the car right now!" Tauheed said as he pointed behind him to Hamids black bmw as they just rounding the SUV, Hamid jumped out of the passenger's seat, leaving the door to his car wide open out of excitement as he realized Esa standing on the other side of that truck, he didn't notice before because he was on his cell phone.

"Esa. Man... when you got out of that truck, I thought that was you then I got an important phone call, but once you started walking around the truck I knew it was you damn man. What's up big bra?" They hugged then Hamid stepped to Shabazz and then they embraced as well as they gave each other the greetings of Peace and once again as they let go Shabazz made yet another comment. "I smell Marijuana". Then he extended his hand to Rasul.

"Rasul." Sul said as the shook hands.

"Your father used to have a lot of your pictures, and always talked about how good you were at football when you were in college, when he would watch us play in the yard in prison."

"Oh.. yeah... That's what up." "Yo E, let me holla at you for a quick sec?" He and Rasul stepped out ear shot. "What's the resume on this dude? I ask because our shit will be coming through Alabama."

"Sul, you know I don't trust people and I'm not try'en to go back to prison. But I'll trust that dude with my life and that's my word son. I swear by Allah."

"Nuff said He can come to the meeting as well. Yo, let's go.. Follow me across the street to the hotel." Rasul said as he looked from Tauheed to Hamid. Shabazz tapped Sul on the shoulder.

"What's up with all that yo stuff… I taught you better than that."

"Come on Pops, stop trippen.. you know I ain't try'na call no shots." Changing the subject just as fast. "We got Siraj, Ashari, and Uncle Hakeem, over there waiting on us." He said as he looked at the Swisstells monogram on the front of the lavish hotel.

"Yo, Esa.. Noooo, not Siraj and Ashari from Chicago, and please tell me you not talking about the brother Hakeem, that was in the wheel chair?"

"Yeah, same people." Esa said with a smile. It looked like Hamid wanted to run across the parking lot as he looked from his old friend to the hotel across the street.

Until Tauheed told him to get in the car so that they could follow the SUV across the street where a Black Mercedes Benz truck with the same color Lincoln Town car was parked idling directly in front of the Hotel's valet parking entrance.

12

"How are you doing today ma'am?" She nodded, then in a deep southern accent with as much hospitality as she could, being caught totally off guard.

"I'm doing just fine, and yourself?"

"I'm not quite sure yet.. what I mean is.. A little thought and some understanding of a situation that really has no real facts.. Because, as all of the evidence is based on speculation and here say, from my understanding of what we all heard over the past month. There were Factious tales, opinions, and lies. Nothing concrete at all. No wire tapped confessions, no hands got caught in the cookie jar, as my grandmother would say, if we got caught doing something wrong. No video or audio surveillance, nor actual witnesses. The only faults our clients have, are the fact that they have all had some type of criminal backgrounds and or been sent to prison on some type of drug charges. Our clients have not only bettered their lives, but they have helped to better the communities around them as well. "People of the jury those defendants were once men without meaning. Now, they've all become men of honor. They have re- established themselves with Non-Profit organizations running within four different cities and states. They've fundraised to open up three different community centers, and five group homes in the current states they resided in. our clients have spent countless hours not only helping, but also talking, caring, and sharing with our youth about better tomorrows, better ways to live, and smarter choice to make. So should they be found guilty of their pasts. For time they have already done? Is it a sin, to have been in trouble with the law? Is it no right turn from negative to positive???"

"Who are we to judge their pasts when their justice was served to them then... The prosecution wants you to believe those defendants sitting;" He points to the defendants table. "Over there, didn't change. What I'm saying is I'm sure but correct me if I'm wrong, that each and every one of us did something in our pasts that we may have regretted at least once in our lives, can we agree?" He again holds his hand up by his side slowly shrugging his shoulders up and down. Now, ladies and gentlemen of the jury comes the help that I've asked you for in the beginning of my closing arguments. Real fast; (with his left hand he pulls out a pocket dictionary from the inside of his suit jackets pocket). I want to look up the word, the prosecution used just before the last witness, was escorted out of the courtroom. "Star witness." He now opens the dictionary and begins to flick thru the pages, where the word star changes to another word, then shows that page to the jury. "That word is not there.. I mean in here look for your selves". He walks back and forth so that every juror could see it.

"Ok being that that word is not in here, lets break the word down and start with the meaning of the word Star; 1: a relatively stationary celestial object visible at night."

"No.. Not that one, now let's try 2: A graphic design with radiating points. No... No.., that's not it either. 3: A superior performer, and 4: a leading actor. "Sounds familiar."

He says as he bats his eye brows at them. "Now let's look up the word Witness." #1:

"One who has seen something. Ahhh it's ok but let's just look a little further to number 2: a sign, Nawww, Number 3. Now this sounds more like what I'm looking for #3: One called upon to testify before the court. Now let's put the words back together again and it's spelled out Clif Harper a.k.a. Preacher man a.k.a. Star Witness. A superior performer and leading actor called to testify before the court."

"Ladies and gentlemen of the jury, this is what's been going on thru out three month long trial. Today the Assistant United States Attorney with yet another ploy using his star performing witness, plus the added pleasures of trying to destroy our clients defamation of character, with today's protection order antics in front of you all. This little incriminating and frivoless act, was yet another stunt to make you, the jury, think that those defendants at that table". He pointed this time looking into each and every jurors eyes very seriously. Are they dangerously stupid and try to bring harm to not just any witness but the prosecutors star witness. Up until now, maybe not even twenty minutes ago Mr. Harper had been living a normal life here in Birmingham Alabama, since his arrest three years ago. No one has of yet said anything remotely harmful to him, but the government all of a sudden now wants you to believe, that his life is now in danger, because of our clients."

"THE MEETING OF THE FAMILY"

13

The first meeting between the family begun, just before 9am on June 5th.8:45am each phone rang from rooms 19c to 19j. The operator told each person who answered their phone to take the elevator up to the penthouse floor Suite L. As each person made their way up to the penthouse, there was a note attached to the door to be left open, and for everyone to Waite in the Executive conference room. Even Rasul, Shabazz, and Esa took the trip up to the lavish top floor of the Swisstell. Wondering what was going on, at 9 o'clock on the dot. Rasul got up, walked out to the front door, then locked it. He came back into the room with a sly smirk on his face. "I am Kiser Sosa." He tried it with a straight face. While everyone looked at him in a what the hec face, until he smiled. "I know everyone was wondering who the heck told them to come up here, well… I had it done, Why? Because I wanted us to be comfortable for the next hour or so. Anyway most you know what's going on. Number 1; We are all equal in our say so's because we all have a voice. Number 2; Trust no one. Number 3; three hundred and sixty four days, is all we have gentlemen, three hundred, sixty, four days… that's all we'll need to get rid of as much cocaine as we can possibly put our hands on. In that 364 days, we will walk away with whatever money we'll have made."

"We'll help each other in every way. If you have anything else to do with drugs of any kind after this time, you will be MURDERED." He looked around the room at each and every one that was in the room sitting at the conference table with a dead serious glare in his eyes. "If not you, only because I can't get to you, it will be someone close to you and it won't stop until we get you. Myself included. I am no exception to these rules. By the three hundredth day we should only be worried about, what where gonna do with all the money and how we're gonna invest it. But until then, stick to Rule number 1. Rule number 4; with 'in this time,, you'll live in the same type of places your already living in, and you'll drive cars no newer than the ones you have already. You'll buy nothing expensive, during this time. If you do, any of these things that I have just mentioned, the same rules apply, as the end of rule 3 states.."

"You and someone you love that's close to will be murdered. Rule number 5; You'll have no direct contact with your street dealers NEVER. They should never know who you are...We've all been in the federal system, so we all know and understand, the risks n stakes are very high, so play this game for keeps. If you need to talk to each other that are in different states, I highly recommend an I'm sure most of you already no to use pay phone to pay phone,, or face to face, and never use the same phone twice in a row. If someone is having a problem with their competition we'll all meet. We'll never let the compaction know what hit them and or their team. Either way they'll become a part of our street team or they'll die as well. It's just that simple. No one ever, never ever meets you under any circumstances. We all will only have one person, that'll know how to contact us, called (the operator)."

"Now, I have a connect that will be given me. My apologies all of us. One cargo container filled with coke. The price tag for the container by the 365th day will cost us one hundred and five million dollars. Our net gross after we finish making our money should be in the ball park of no less than fifteen million dollars apiece, after everyone else gets paid. Which brings the grand total gross to two hundred and twenty five million dollars."

"Siraj: Big Bruh. I already know that you have total control over your mid-west section especially having high standards with the G's, the china white will be brought to you as much as you can handle, and you'll be able to rid it off at your price.

"Ashari: The same goes for you, you can get rid of it at 17.5. No one will beat that tag right now, I'm sure you'll have connects coming out of the wood works looking for our product. Because it's coming in un cut we'll do all the stepping on it when it does.

"Hakeem: Unk... I got people from Baltimore on down, I even got someone for you to meet. His name is Saheed, he's from east B-more, he can be your front man if you like let me no after you meet him. He Doesn't mind killing and making money most important he's a very loyal dude. You'll have from the Mason Dixie line thru the Carolinas." "You".. Rasul then pointed to Hamid who's atoms apple now looked like it was caught in his throat, when Sul pointed to him, catching him completely by surprise. "The container will be coming through a port in Alabama. I'll give you the time and place.. Note.. it'll be at any givin moment. 'Got me' Just be ready and on point once we leave this room today."

"What do you want me to do?"

"You'll receive some money from my father, to open up a store near our safe houses. Not rent from but buy so we can blow it up if we please. One of our houses only you and my father will know about. That's the one where everything will be. The second one will be the wrap house. One of us will call you, then someone will meet you there, to pick up our orders. Do you have someone you can trust. I'm not asking you do you think you have someone. "NO" DO YOU HAVE SOMEONE WHO YOU REALLY TRUST? To move some bricks thru the dirty south."

"He got me." Tauheed said.

"No, not you Ty your role is the most important. We'll be sending and bringing you All of the money. I trust you'll have no paper trail, being that you were once a vice president of a very lucrative investment bank. Remember… Everything must go to off shore accounts."

"You do understand me when I tell you everything. You and my father will work together, always direct contact."

"Esa. fam.. You've always been my other half. You'll keep your daily routine, but your nights will mostly belong to me while Sha thinks you're at work. We'll run as far up as Boston, to which I've already hollered at Black and Suge (G). We got the green light, their already waiting on us and as for New Haven I also hollered at old crazy behind Kenya and her sister Michelle, we both know they sexy ass get that money. We got dog in Harlem, and D-nice and his brother Douge from Suger Hill in Jersey, at the bottom we got R- base in Wilmington Delaware, feel me. Listen fellas we can.. Move this stuff fast."

"Believe me. No excess spending for one year, is all I ask, and stay low, never let your right hand no what your left hand is doing, seriously never let anyone know you're coming or going. Meaning your underbosses. Very important and seriously don't let them know when this is over. We all know that casualties come with war. I say that to say' when this is finished, all underbosses have to become expendable. So when you choose that person, know that he has only three hundred and sixty five more days from the day we start."

"When is that." Hamid said.

"When I pop up on you, where ever you are, just start counting from that very moment! We'll all help each other cause at the end of the day, it's like a pizza pie.

We will split it eight ways. "Any more questions!"

"How am I gonna get the money... Not by mail right?"

"Right. All the paper (Money) will be brought directly to you. You'll be notified in a sufficient amount of time before hand, plus my father." Rasul put his hands on the back of his father's shoulders while Shabazz was still seated. "He'll be down this way near you, it's too hot for him up North. He's gonna stay low. We'll open up some kind of clothing stores down here, he's extremely good at retail. Guess that's why where here today" he said with a chuckle. One here in Atlanta, and the other one in Alabama, so going into the stores won't look out of place. "Brothers." As Esa said to me coming down here. This can be something special. I love all of you. Whatever you need, from me it will be done, if it's in my power."

"Pop's! Please pass me that bag over there." Shabazz looked puzzled at the bag. Then stated more to himself than anyone else.

"If I was a gambling man, I'd bet that, that was the same bag that I carried off of the plane." He was thinking as he walked over to the bag. "You mean this one."

He pointed to the bag on the other end of the table.

" Yes that's it!" Sul put the garment bag on the table, he then unzipped it, pulled out a few college size Webster's Dictionaries and laid them on the table.

"I thought those felt like books." Were his father's thoughts once again a little louder under his breath than even he expected. With a letter opener, he cut across, then down both sides of the binding areas of the books. Then pulled to tightly wrapped blocks from the fake dictionaries. Cut them open with the letter opener, then separated eight stacks of new one hundred dollars bill bundles, as he picked up one of the stacks he tossed it to each individual person until only one was left on the table.

"Each stack contained fifty thousand dollars, you may do as you please with it. It's a token of good faith from me to you all. We might as well have some fun before the work begins."

" Dj Cutt, and Dj Quest, are down here from Paterson. Hamm from Sugar Hill got CakeBossCancune preforming this weekend. New Jersey rockin' at Club 112 tonight, and Levels Night Club tomorrow it's up to you guys."

"Oh yeah.. Tawheed, I apologize for being so rude. You've already met my cousin and my father." Sul walked over, and around the table to put one hand on Siraj's shoulder, then the other one on Ashari's shoulder. "These two are also my real brothers," then walked passed his brothers to the man in the wheel chair. This is my Uncle Hakeem n it's only God's blessings that he's still around... Hamid sat in shear stunned silence, until it was too much for him to hold in. "You mean to tell me all that time we did together .. I .. I knew you guys were close, but not that close!"

"Let me answer that Rasul." His father said. "Son that's how our family moves. We protect each other that way, when everyone knows your family, they tend to look for the person in charge or the point man."

"When they don't know, and think we're just friends, they sometimes slip and say things telling on themselves. Then we crush them! You understand me now." We move like panthers in this jungle call life."

"That's why this meeting was called. When my son said earlier to not let your left- hand know what your right hand is doing. Do you understand this is how we have to move. We have no other options. The risks and stakes in this thing are too high."

"We'll all be facing too much time ant to factual there's a good chance we will all be facing twenty years and or up to a life sentence!"

"Yeah.. I guess so." "Good, now I can go get me some sleep, my son has had me up for almost two days. Please excuse me brothers. If I'm needed for further assistance, I will be in my room." Shabazz fixed his glasses on his noise then looked at his room key as if it was foreign. I'm in room 19e, ok brothers. "As sallamu Alaikum."

"Wa laikum as Sallam," all the brothers said in unison.

14

The lead officer couldn't believe what he had just saw and who he was looking at, as he moved in closer and stood over the man. Another deep confusion swept through him, with disbelief and an unwanted but broken trust. It was his pastor, Pastor Cliff Harper, from the 6th Avenue Baptist Church. The same person who'd married his two children of and what was more hurtful. He was the same person he'd heard just a marvelous sermon from not even several hours ago, about trusting in the Lord and respecting your own dignity thru patience. After a stunned second of rattled thoughts.

"Put your clothes on slow and keep hands where I can see them." As he spoke to the pastor of his church, his partner noticed the confused look in his commanding officers eyes.

"Sarg, I think we got something over here." It was a sandwich size glassine package of what looked like a cocaine substance.

"This can't be happening to me. I don't believe this. How am I gonna explain this… to my wife." His thoughts rolled on. "We trusted you for over twenty-five years, we stood with you when the Church got bombed and those innocent young girls who were killed from the explosion." Sargs, thoughts kept jumping from past to present.

"Sir. Can I please speak with you outside for a second."

"Yeah.. come on.. I need some air."

"Sarg, are you alright! You look like you saw a ghost or something? And the guy really looks familiar, do you know him Sir?"

"Yes Mat.. I know him very well or so I thought… I still can't believe what I just saw."

"I'm sure you noticed this second trailer, behind this one. In it is about 65,000 pounds of cocaine for you to do what you have to do in the time you need, if you feel you may need more, like I told you I need like 2/3 days tops, but I think that's a crazy number in there already, in you need me for any reason, please don't hesitate to call me ANYHING. No one knows what's in that trailer but us three, all these other vehicles have very big stash spots with directions to all of them, in the glove boxes."

"Oh yeah, not sure if you need that pickup truck." Carlos pointed to in the far left corner. "To run a round in besides the jeep you could, its tuned up, runs good but it doesn't have a stash box in it. We was using it to move lawn equipment around when we first got started, with that business. "Keys in the ash tray."

"That's all I need to know." He said as he handed the bag to his brother. "How long you up here for Los."

"How long you need me up here."

"Just until tomorrow, show us around a little, maybe slid to motor vehicle with us in the morning, then go over these stash spots in these vehicle's, because I'm sure this is all your work, and that's just about it."

"Ok that's no problem I'll stay up here for a few days if need be."

"Aiight cool that's a plus." He said looking at his brother, then back at Los. "Man now let's go get something to eat, Shit me and Big Bruh aint eat nothing today but a cup of Dunkin donuts coffee."

"Man I was wondering when we was gonna eat something". His brother said to him."

"Yo I guess we can get a room at that hotel we passed getting of the exit going to his place."

"Bruh he ain't even from here he from Miami? This whole shit just went over my head, This the dude you was in Atlanta United States Penitentiary with?"

"Yeah…" Rasul said.

"Ooh man, my bad my dude lill bruh used to talk about you all the time when he first came home." He extended his hand once again, this time when Carlos went to shake it Melv, drew him in for more of a family hug. "Yo, why you ain't say this was dude."

"I figured you would catch on sooner or later." He said not being smart, but being real.

"Why yall gonna stay at a hotel when yall got two houses I gonna bring you to see once we get something to eat."

"Man, we gotta get some furniture first Los, you buggen."

"Naw Sul the second house is fully furnished, the family sold it with everything in it. I made them an offer that they couldn't refuse. Even the first house is halfway done I had brought some stuff over there one day when I saw the for sale sign across the street."

"Oh Okay, next question, we need some heat down here."

"Already done, two 40 cals, in the stash box of the Cherokee, an AR15 with extended clips and two more 9mm's, under the back steps of the second house."

"Damn Los," Man you got all the bases covered, I really appreciate you bruh."

"Sul I wouldn't be home, right now if it wasn't for you." "Now let's go eat." He said as they were now right in front of the SUV that they pulled up in. getting back into the same doors that they had gotten out of.

"Who is he Sarg ?"

"It's Mr. Harper from the 6th Avenue Baptist Church."

"No disrespect Sir.. but isn't that the church where you and your wife attends?"

"Yes Mat. let's go back inside and take care of this situation. Mat… was that real dope you found?"

"Yes Sir," he said to his senor officer not so energized because of the bond he had with his superior officer and friend. "It's about $800 worth.. sarg, that's a lot for someone to say it's personal use. Plus the young lady is saying that she has no I.D. on her so we'll have to bring her in as well."

"Let me talk to him, when we get back in there ok, Matty. I really need to make some sense of this situation."

"Ok. Sarg." They opened the door to see both suspects fully dressed and cuffed sitting on the edge of the first twin bed nearest the door. The man was weeping to the point of uncontrollable ness. The girl on the other hand, after the initial shock of it not being robbers, but cops, she just sat there lost in space, and by her reactions, you can tell she was very much high off of the narcotics she had induced.

"Sarg.. can we talk? Please.. Sir, we need to talk. Please let me.. Look.. I know this doesn't look right or good, but those drugs". He pointed to them while one of the other officers were holding the plastic bag. "were here when we got here."

"I know I'm very wrong for being with this lady." The pastor said as he looked at what used to be an almost lifelong friend. "Stan.. Please listen to me." As the preacher now standing and shaking half to death, weeping, as he was talking.

"You've known me for over thirty years, Stan… please say something to me." The commanding officer looked from one officer to another then back at his old friend and Pastor, as his focus still kept slipping in and out.

"You sir, have the right to remain silent." Then finished of reading him his miranda rights.

"We'll talk at the station house, you may want a lawyer present." It was the last thing that was said as two other officers walked the man and the young lady, out of the room down the hall to the elevator. The officer pushed it's button the charm rang out, then the door opened. As they stepped in one of the officers had them face the rear of the elevator as they road down then off of it, though the main lobby out of the front of the hotel with one escort in the front and one in the back of the dual, to the on waiting patrol cars.

The next morning after the brothers left motor vehicle with their new identities, Rasul's first call was to his father, then his close cousin Esa, letting them know, that his dreams have just become reality just as he called the rest of his family to make preparations for the days to come, because come hell or hot water it's no turning back now. Every one sounded so excited, but his brother Big Melv, was the most pumped because not only was he a ghost rider in this whole thing, with no one but Rasul knowing he was all the way, his younger brother promised to split his share down the middle.

" Damn bruh, I'm not sure what you done for dude bruh, but that load at that warehouse ain't none of us ever seen that kind of money, at one shot. Not even pop's. So what next"?

" We gonna put, Lill Oak, Quan, and Troub, on a plane to come here in a couple of days, oh yeah Mas too need his crazy ass down here to keep your hands from getting dirty, cause he don't mine putting in that work. Anyway there gonna think you and ole girl, missed the flight, coming in on the next one. Same dude who came an got us from the airport, gonna bring them to the Ramada Inn right across the street from the University of South Alabama, so they don't look out of place, there will be three rooms reserved. They get two, plus yours on another floor, just for the night. When they think you'll be arriving that night, you can put like a $1,000 (stack) in their pockets, to run a round with for a few days. You know.. Get used to things going on around here. Next morning you can bring them to the safe house it's like five bed rooms, they got enough money to by the little things they may need because it's already queen size beds in all the rooms. I want them to think you're staying with ole girl down here by the school somewhere when you'll actually be staying across the street, watching everything they'll be doing, after we step up these cameras. The space in between these houses, with all these trees and stuff is amazing because with the tints on the pickup, and the fact that you can drive out the back of the second house instead of the front, they won't even pay any attention to the truck even having the jeep back there as well, when they think you spending time with ole girl.

"They can use the uniforms and medical vans to move things around the south, holla at Los about ID's for them, so no bodies using their real names down this way. Plus we got the Rig to move things further north Feel me."

"I feel you.. Now what about the factory?"

"Let's move like10,000 pounds at a time to the second house now. Keep like 2500 bricks (kilos) at the safe, at all times. The way our properties are set up, you can act like you going to meet with the connect by disappearing across the street for a couple hours, plus you can keep an eye on what's going on across the street. Call me each time you ready another load. I'll fly down the night before, we move the stuff early in the morning. O yeah I was just looking at my phone for a Radio Shack so we can go pick up some extra wireless cameras to put around the house, there's two already for the front and back door that's hidden already, I want like three more in the house and 2 outside, we can put in the trees somewhere, plus two outside your spot so you can keep an eye on your outer perimeters by remote, and I also can keep an eye on the safe house from up top. I saw a utility ladder in that pickup truck yesterday."

"Okay let's get to it. Let's go get the pickup truck first, shoot across the street to that Super Walmart pick up some sweats, groceries, and some things for both the houses, then to Radio Shack, in that order."

"I'm cool with that, but we might have to stop at Best Buy cause I ain't staying there another night without a television in my room."

"Your room…. Man you ain't even gonna be down here like that and you know it."

"Ok watch and see. I bet I'll be down here more that you know it."

"Yeah aiight, we'll see." Melv said as he jumped in the passenger seat, Rasul was rounding the Jeep Cherokee to hop in the driver's seat while he was punching numbers in his phone, then put it to his ear.

"Hello.. Yeah what's good? Yo we gonna shoot down to that Walmart, and Radio Shack grab a few things, to help my man get these places in a little order, we gon hit you up a lill later, aiight bruh? Bet peace". Then he hit the end button on his phone.

Almost eight in a half hours later, as he was resting across his bed half dreaming, he thought his heart was giving out, until it nervously jarred him fully awake. As he sat up he realized, it wasn't his heart, but his cell phone vibrating. As he opened it he quickly recognized the number, and pushed the answer button.

"Hello." He said in a half sleep raspy voice.

"Damn mann, Yo you good?" Been trying to reach you for almost two hours. Just making sure you ok that's all, I know y'all knew to these parts, didn't know what was going on."

"We just cleaned up both places real good, before we start grooving feel me."

"Okay, okay just checking on you I'm pulling out tomorrow just wanted to see if y'all wanted to grab a bit to eat ain't no tell when imma see you again any time soon."

"Okay, we can do it, I'll be over your way in about 15/20 minutes.

15

June 5th, 1997. Friday, One year to the date later,

The family was given everything they needed for what was supposed to be the rest of their lives, which in turn brought them all over the top. After they paid off their connect, in a grand total of, One hundred and ten million dollars, five of which was a bonus to the connect for affording the family the chance and opportunity, plus the trust factor that was given with no strings attached, besides the fact that the person who set up the deal with his past supplier, sat down with Rasul on two occasions. The first was a meeting with his connect at the St. Regis Hotel in New York City, NY.

"I heard you've only had a couple small complications "Sul."

"Yeah well… we took care of the few situations as they accrued. In a few day's we'll have everything else taken care of. Everyone that was directly linked to us has already disappeared. Here's the codes and security numbers you'll need for all your money. "Los… the family truly thanks you for everything. Here's a little token of our loyalty for your services." Rasul handed him yet another set of numbers.

" What's this?"

"These numbers are also yours, we put an extra five million dollars in another account, just in case one of us got into any real complications and had to disappear.

It's now yours my friend.. The family has given you a total of one hundred and ten million dollars.

"Thanks Sul"

"No.. Thank you Carlos for everything. Damn son… Remember when we first met in Federal prison working in drapery at that dug on Unicor in Atlanta.. I never thought that this day would ever come. When you called me and told me that you won your appeal, I was truly happy for you.. Then when you called me and asked me about my 365 day plan, that I spoke to you about a couple times, I wasn't sure if it would really work in that short of time span, but the numbers your people gave you made us all a lot of money.. I've been curious to know about how much money you made off this, but it's truly none of my business. Me and my family are happy with what we got, "real talk." As Sul stood up to leave Carlos held out his hand, then asked Rasul to wait.

"Yo Sul…Damnn please don't rush out of here, you act like we ain't old friends and we'll forever be close like brothers, you do know that right? Because once you leave here I'll be on my way back to Miami. I have to go home for a few weeks, then I'll be going on a nice vacation, to holla at a few of my people in Columbia. Sul I say this to say.. we've made a lot of money together, if you ever." Rasul cut him off in the mid-sentence raising both hands from side to side in a please stop gesture.

"No more." Never.. I love you big bruh but it's over for me and my family and as a matter of fact. One of my partners that live in

Alabama, just sent me the keys to both safe houses by the ports. If you want those properties. There yours, I'll send you the keys. There good hiding spots, only me, him and my father know where they are."

"Los," I don't care to remember. I'll send you that info with the keys, and security codes to ur contact spot ok."

"Sul.. Now let me finish talking you still ain't change." He said with a half chuckle.

"Before you cut me off again, I was saying if you ever need me for anything at any time and place, please call me, even if you need to get away from everything.."

"This game is my life right now, as you no, I don't plan on going back, I plan on holding court in the streets, if need be."

"I feel you Los. Thank you again bruh for your extended hand to me and my family… But I'm sorry. As long as your still in the game, I'll have to stay away.. Now with no disrespect. Please forgive me, my cousin Esa is waiting for me out side. We now have to finish our clean-up process."

"Sul, man.. I could really use you as my right hand man, I really mean it everything, 50/50 all the way around the board. You're a heartless dude. Ha, Ha, Ha."

Carlos chuckles as he walks up to Rasul and gives him a big bear hug. "Call me.."

"Let me know what yawl did with all that cash."

"I will give you my word Los, I'll check in on you from time to time.. You be safe. I know you said you'll hold court in the streets, but you got a lot of snakes out there ready to bite that ass the first chance they get, even family will set that ass up properly gassed up, feel me.. I don't even trust my shadow because when it rains it disappears if u understand what I'm saying." Rasul then turned and headed from the penthouses massive living quarters. Carlos picked up his global encrypted cell phone, punched in a few numbers, waited until another voice came on the line. Los was a cool brother from day county, Miami Florida, He stood about 5'10, brown skinned well dressed and always war a bald head with a full neatly trimmed beard, a little on the cubby side, he spoke fluent Spanish from growing up around Cubans most of his life. Learned the game, became heartless after watching his father die a violent death right in front of him, an once he became a part of the game he played for keeps and always kept that deadly smile on his face to which most women thought it was a cute smirk because of his one dimple.

"Olah.. here's the numbers to the accounts in the Caymans'. I sent your seventy five, plus my thirty together. Please separate it then send my share to my account in St. Lucia. Then call a travel agent for two tickets to the Caribbean Islands, you pick a spot it doesn't matter just need somewhere to kick back for a few days, and think.

Then call me back as soon as you handle this. Carlos pressed the end button on his phone, laid it down on the Bottega Veneta Low-slug coffee table. He walked out onto the lugubrious Balcony. Two minute later, he watched his old prison buddy walk out of the Hotel, jump into the passenger seat of a red range rover 4.6, lower his window halfway then drive off down 5th Avenue. Made a quick right hand turn and disappeared into the heavy traffic.

"Damn Sul.. If I could form a team like the one you have, I might try my hand at the same move… Naw I'm cool, I won't know what to do with myself, when I'm done. I'd be bored." Were Carlos's thoughts as he headed back into the suite to pack his thins for his trip back south.

16

M at followed alongside the sergeant as they exited the second elevator.

"Sarg., Do you want me to see which vehicle these keys belong to, and tow it away from here to the station and do a little checking thru it.. We did find all that coke in his room?"

"Yes Mat.. because I don't see Pastor Harpers car in this lot anywhere, they had to get here somehow son". He said as they then stood out in front of the Ramada Inn with both his hands on his hips. It was about several hours later around 2:45 in the morning now, since the commanding officer took statements from both the suspects, and now almost finishing up his reports for the night on this matter at hand.

"Sarg, you have a call on line four, from a Federal Agent Lewis.."

"Thank you Dian, send it through."

"Yes, Sergeant Thomas... am I correct?" Before really giving the officer a real chance to answer him, he went on. "How are you doing this morning. Can we talk.. I mean are you busy right now?"

"Yeah this is Thomas.. how are you... Agent Lewis is it? What can I do for you this morning."

"You arrested someone earlier tonight. A Clif Harper." The Sergeant almost dropped the phone, that was laid cradled between his shoulder and ear, and flipped backwards out of the old wooden swivel chair he was just resting and thinking in, at the mention of his pastors name. More confusion started clouding his brain once again and wasn't getting any better especially with this phone call. He hadn't even had the chance with so much going on, to call home and check in on his family as of yet. His regular shifts hour were well passed his time to go home. He was actually waiting on the setting of the bail from the Majesty Judge. He'd been at the station house all night trying to sort things out with his old friends conflicting stories, then finding out the young lady that was in the hotel room was never the les a minor, now this crap!

"Sergeant... are you still on the line!"

"Yes.. I'm still here.. what can I do you the pleasure of?"

"I just need you to keep him away from every one if possible, because we need to come speak with him."

"Ok.. will do, come on over.. I'm sure you'll shed some light on this." He said more to himself than the Agent as they both said thanks to each other disconnected then the Agent shouted something, as he pulled the phone back to his ear. Once again he leaned back in his chair, folded his hands into each other behind his head as his thoughts started to race on where fast, and to think, I thought I knew this man, all this time he's been trying to spill his gutts to me all night, just hoping he would get out of here before morning, now the FEDs want to speak to him? I've personally made sure that no one even knows he's in our custody as of yet! Jesus what next? Let me go check on Matty, I'm sure he's just as tired as I am".

"Did you guys impound a vehicle, that was at the hotel?"

"Yes.. we have it here at the station."

"Good, we'll be there in about one hour. I have to brief my supervisor and director."

"Oh yeah.. did he tell you guys anything about the smuggling ring"?

"What!" "What smuggling ring.. Agent Lewis." now sitting fully erect in his chair now.

"We went to the hotel, because someone called our 911 dispatcher, to report a possible shots being fired." He stated with so much confusion, he clearly sounded pissed off.

"We'll talk when we get there sargent face to face.. Your percent's phones are not secure lines". The phone went dead. He held the phone cradled to his ear for about another five seconds before he hung the phone up. As he pushed himself back, from his desk with his feet, and raised both arms to massage his temples, then leaned back in his swirl chair with both hands intertwined behind the nap of his head and neck area.

"Man.." He said to himself as he closed his eyes. "All these years.. It's crazy when you think you know someone, then you find out that you don't really know them at all. I pray that all that stuff he was telling me while we were in that cell talking together wasn't bullshit, "Jesus Christ," and whatever this drug ring is this federal agent is talking about. I just can't wait until this night is all over with… Man I really need some rest from all this wow."

꒰

April 1st, 1999. 6am in the morning. Ring, ring, ring.

"Baby, can you get my cell phone for me? tell who ever it is I'll call them back when I get out of the shower, ok."

"Ok, Bae." Not even two minutes later, Rasul's wife walked into the bathroom.

"Baby, it's someone named Carlos.. He said he's a good friend of yours.. He said it's very important Very, very important!" Sul opened the showers with water wallowing out everywhere. He reached for his phone with one hand, with soap all over him, as the hand turned off the dual shower heads.

"Hello."

"Yo Sul! I really need to see you bruh.. "Like now!" It's very important."

"Calm down Los… What's really good?"

"I need to see you.. No phones, "Feel me."

"I feel you. Ok when and where?"

"Today.. I should be landing in Teteboro shortly."

"Huh?" "Listen Big bruh… I'll meet you at the airport.." Sul tossed the phone back to his half nude beautiful light skinned /caramel complexation skin toned wife, as he grabbed one of the towels on the rack next to the shower.

"Bae what's wrong?" What's going on? and where are you going?"

"I thought you were gonna bring the baby to the nursery today for me?"

"Sheema. Bae... Something very important just came up. Please. Please, I need for you to drop him off on your way to work ok, please." He said as he looked at his wife's beautiful puppy dog eyes, that now looked half filled with water from worry, as she's always worried about him since he's been home, because it took a little over a decade for him to come home from federal prison. Before he left she thought she'd never see him again. She was young at the time they met at a night club in New York called "Speed." To which she then ran into him again in her home town in New Jersey where they met again, but this time they hooked up and started dating, she never really knew much about him in the streets, with the exception of the stories she heard in the streets about his wild ways, but with the long talks they'd share at night, she saw a different person from the man they talked about and told her to leave him alone.

It wasn't long before she fell in love with him, and the craziest thing happened that same night she called him and first told him she loved him. He was snatched off the streets and out of her life, and the look her husband had in his eyes clearly told her something was wrong.

"I'm not sure.. but I'll call you once I find out ok. "I promise."

"Sul... Who's Carlos?"

"He's an old friend from my past life.. Bae I don't have time to explain now, but once I do you'll know who he is too me. Please Bae.. No more questions, Ok."

"You better call me at work and let me know that you're ok... I haven't seen that look on your face in a few years, baby please be safe."

"I will. I promise..." Sul said as he was now rushing and throwing his clothes on as he half ran out of the house, with soap still in one ear. He jumped into his silver Mercedes s600. Backed out of his driveway with screeching tires headed for Teteboro, Airport. After the three hundred and sixty five days Rasul moved his family from New York to the suburbs of New Jersey, where his wife once lived. He only lived about 5 minutes from the George Washington Bridge, which separates New York City from New Jersey. Then, jumped on U.S. Highway Route 46 west from his home in Fort lee, NJ.

Now in the direction to the airport, it only took him 10 minutes weeding in and out of the early morning traffic as he made the left-hand turn down Teteboro road, heading towards the private air strips entrance. Once he pulled into the entrance gate he drove about another twenty-five yards Sul swung his car around beside hanger #14. He then watched the runway after he noticed, there was no signs of life in the hanger until almost five minutes later a Golf stream 200 made his landing now speeding down the track to a quick slow-down headed in his direction. The Learjet pulled into hanger Sul was parked beside. He then exited his vehicle, and walked toward the plane, as the dual engines were throttling down. As he reached the plane, the side door opened out with the stairs unfolding down the side of the jet, Sul didn't wait for anyone to exit as he climbed the few steps two at a time, then ducked into the small craft.

"Shit must have hit the fan somehow," were his thoughts because Carlos would never have called me for a meeting out of the blue like this. Now looking to his left at the pilot, then to his right where Los was engaged in what a phone conversation with someone who must have been very important, because it looked heated and the look on his face told me it didn't look good as he put his index finger up in a one moment gesture but it actually took another three minutes before he hung up his cell phone with a bewildered look on his face, then slammed his cell phone on the mahogany lavish desk his elbows rested on.

"What the hell happened last night?" Sul.. We got a problem.. A big problem, some dude whose name is Cliff Harper, also known as Preacherman, aka Mr. lucky charm was arrested about two days ago, and he's spilling his gutts to the alphabet boys."

"I don't understand… what the hell that got to do with me los?"

"It's has a lot to do with you! Especially when he's saying your families (B.B.O.P.) Organization is controlling most of the cocaine that's coming thru the south."

"Whattt… I aint do'en shittt! Yo who is that mother F^?k..?"

" Sul.. Pump your brakes.. We know you and your guys are all legit now, I'm not saying that. He named someone. A "Hamid Baxtor". You know him?"

"Yeah. That's one of my partners from Alabama."

"Yeah.. I know that too." How? Because I just know things! Anyway this dude Preacher Man was released to set up one of my Lieutenants last night. He flipped as well. I'm not sure just how much info he's told the FEDs and ATF, but what I do know is he was the one your men Hamid Baxter would meet to move the coke across state lines. He was actually the one that brought your guys some of their shit" Here's a picture of him, "Know him?"

"Naw.. Me and my cousin would never meet the drop man. You remember the last meeting we had in New York. I told you I would get rid of anyone leading back to me. "Well guess I didn't?" I'm not sure if my uncle or if my dudes from Chicago met your guy, but we can definitely find out right now!" Get your pilot to fly us into Chi-town". Carlos got up from his seat and walked into the cockpit. He spoke with the pilot for a few minutes then returned.

"He needs to refuel and get something to eat."

"How long Los?"

"He needs one hour, I told him we're in the air in that hour. He'll be ready."

"Damn.. Shit.. Let me see if I can call Ashari first. Their an hour behind us central time, hopefully he's still in his house." After the fourth ring his son picked up, the house phone.

"Hello."

"Can I speak to Ashari."

"Who dis?"

"Tell him it's Sul, and I really need to speak to him, Ok."

"Hey Unk.. hold on Uncle Sul." A couple seconds later.

"What's good bruh? Asalaamu Alaikum"

"Wa laikum Asalaamu. I need to meet with you and big bra!"

"When?"

"Now!" I'll be there in a couple of hours, like around 10am your time."

"Wooooo.. What's going on?"

"Not on the phone Ak. It's very important. I need to show you and Big bra something. Do you know if he's home?"

"I don't think he's home, he may be at one of the community centers we're supposed to speak to some of the kids this morning got a new summer program going, because we have a tournament coming next week, but right now this maybe more important."

"You really don't understand, this may mean our freedom!"

"Our WHAT!!!!"

"I got your attention, I'm glad you understand me now". I'll be in the air in minute. Which community center?"

"The one we have on the Southside off of Atlantic."

"Ok.. I'll meet both of you there, peace beloved." Rasul said as he pushed the end button on his phone, then started pacing the isle. "Los.. where's your lieutenant at now?"

"The FEDs still have him, but my sources tell me he's gonna get out on bail to assist the Government and help the Feds set people up." So I'm sure you know me and your Family are the targets!"

17

Beginning of the Summer 1996 Birmingham-Shuttlesworth International Airport. Day 360.** Sunny skies, a temperature just under 98 degrees, but the humidity made it feel like it was 109 degrees in the shade, as Rasul walked out of the Arrivals terminal, then hopped into a black jeep Cherokee, with the air conditioner blasting on high for the next 3 in a half hours.

"What's good bruh." Melv said as his younger brother hopped into the front passenger seat, giving each other a half hug considering the console was between them.

"Man." Rasul said with long sigh. "Big bruh we did it. "We rich, after we clean up down here, it's over." It's really over big burh. He said a second time, as he leaned his head back until it pushed back against the head rest as his eyes, now fixed straight out the front window, of the SUV as they cruised down the interstate, in silence for almost an hour.

"Whatcha wanna do first, the houses or the vehicles?"

"We did the vans already. Mas, Quan, and Lill Oak, boarded their plane at 11:30 this morning, which was perfect timing, picking you up

I only waited about twenty-five minutes, Troub wanted to ride with me but because you didn't answer your phone this morning, He down by the college."

"Down by what college?"

"Man all them dudes had broads at the college."

"Oh really."

"Yeah, but Troub fell in love, he's been staying on campus with her for the past month or so. I told him it was time to go when I made the reservations for everyone else, but he asked me can I make his for tomorrow evening, he said he even had a ride there so I was like aiight cool, and made it for then."

"He don't know I'm down here right?"

"Did you really just ask me that question, when you've been down here how many times, like 20/30 times, and no one ever knew but me."

It was almost 5am, in the morning, when the government agents arrived at the station house in dark colored suits. There was one other person in tow with the agents who wasn't wearing a suit, in fact he was wearing a soft cream colored cashmere sweater with dark brown slacks and gold horn rimmed glasses. Once the five agents reached the sergeants desk, the younger Tom Cruise looking fella with the gold horned glasses stepped forward.

"I am Assistant United States Attorney Michael Kelly." He held out his hand to the commanding officer. They shook hands.

"What can I do for you guys." The Sarg said. Another officer stepped up.

"I am Agent Alvin Lewis.. I spoke with you on the phone." First!! Segant Thomas, was it.. Can you please have someone show these two." He pointed to two other agents that were standing next to him that backed off once the A.U.S.A. stepped forward.

"Yes I can, Mat. Hey Mat.. Can you please show these." He pointed. "Two agents to where that suv is that we towed in tonight from the hotel."

"Yes, Sir.. Right away, Sarg." As Mat walked away with the two agents in tow, one of them stopped, and reached down for what looked like a tool box.

"Can someone please explain what's going on here?" The Sergeant said.

"Sure." Said, the United States Attorney. "We've been running a 3 yearlong investigation sting along with D.E.A and A.T.F. and other local law enforcements, in several different Southern States to which have been running from the Florida Keys, up thru Maryland, and your Mr. Clif Harper, aka Preacher man aka Mr. Lucky charm, also known as the man that your currently holding in your lockup was on our raid list yesterday, at that same hotel, just a few hours before you guys arrested him. He's a Major mule for the "Ross crime family." We've already locked up a Lucious Boswell aka Lucious Banana. "You heard of him?"

"No.. No I don't think that rings a bell no, why.. should I?"

"Well he's a top dog in the family, and an extremely ruthless bastard. He was set up by his Capo, a Mr. Tony V. yesterday who's now a cooperating witness for the government they're from a small town in the Madison area of Georgia. Now they've taken over most Atlanta up to the Rocky Mountain North Carolina area with their low priced cocaine trade. We'll have Mr. Banana's Capo tone v back out on the streets working for us in a couple of days, were currently working out the red tape with his federal judge. Mr. Boswell doesn't know that his capo flipped as of yet."

"Tone v. keeps telling us about someone by the name of "Carlos." Who's cocaine headquarters and empire is all over the 305 Miami area in Liberty City. But this Carlos is a ghost right now mostly like a myth to all of our ci's and cw's down there because no one knows who he is and or what he looks like if that is his real name we're not sure of that either. With the exception of Mr. Lucious Banana Boswell or Banana as he's called in the streets won't talk to any of us about anything, this guy is really loyal to whomever this Carlos person is and he's one of the few who really knows who Carlos Ross really is. He knows he's facing a life sentence because of the amount of cocaine we busted his capo with n were not letting him breathe right now no phone calls or anything until we talk to your guy Mr. Harper because we don't know just how deep this situation goes. He may not know anything but were not taking any chances as of yet Sargent Thomas. But we do know we need our witness Tone V. back on the streets and if we can get Mr. Harper to cooperate as well, we'll have them work together with all our agencies to help take down the "Ross family" and lock them away forever. Ok. So let's go speak to this lucky charm guy and see what he knows."

"I ain't mean it like that". It's just that our time has been over down here for a little over about a month ago, and they still stayed down here. " Shit they got there 50grand apiece as promised to them last month. Come to think about it they all walked away with at least a hundred grand total give or take. I wanted to come then, to get this over with". I ain't tell Los we done yet, because we ain't. I still got two people on this list, that gotta get missing, I explained to them at our first meeting, that casualties come with war, and whomever their front men weren't supposed to let their right hand know what their left hand was doing, but these two clowns, can possibly decapitate us, and the sad part on their end is they don't even know we know. The dude that picks up for Siraj, did a pick up the last couple times with a new dude, now this new guy came up with an idea, to rob the next drop, but what they don't know is there is no next drop, and because he brought somebody new with him they both gonna die tonight, they staying in a slum motel, with 2 stripper chicks right off the freeway, coming into this city. The brother from down this way got wind of it a wanted to make the move himself, but I asked him to wait until I get down here because I'm tryna find out just how much they know before, they take their last breath."

"I don't want him to see your face because we look to much alike. You've been practically the biggest part of this whole operation, The ghost of everything that needed to be done from down this end. You made sure it was handled. Clean and swift. It's time for you to take a break. How much money we got left to send to Pop's."

"To be exact it's a little over 39 million."

" 39."What? "What's the total you sent pop's way?" Do you know off hand?"

"Damn bruh what you think I'm trya beat you or something?"

"Hell no, just asking."

"I think after the last run the total was about 2 hundred and 44 tickets. I'll tell you the exact number, when we get to the house." That's crazy yo."

"What's crazy."

"You Bruh.. you don't trust me."

"Man your way off the mark, imma show you just how much I trust you once we get to the spot and we have that number you say you sent."

"What the heck is that supposed to mean."

"Don't be stupid bro, I'm not talking like that you buggin." "Anyway imma need you to drop me off in the pickup after he calls me sometime around 11. When we done I'm gonna have him drop me off down by the student center, I'll text you beforehand so you can already be there cause I would hate to mess around and run into Troub, down here."

"Aiight." His brother said in a I'm no longer beat for this conversation voice.

"Imma meet with Carlos in New York, next week some time." Don't forget from here I gotta fly to Atlanta, to meet with the Family. Imma have them meet me there on friday, so we got a couple days. I wanna get them vans painted all black, and detailed, then have them hipped back uptop, I got plans for them."

"What about this jeep."

"You can keep it, if you want."

"Hell no! You know what I want. I wanted that big rig since day one."

"Okay it's yours.. Who said you couldn't have it."

"Naw, I just thought you was giving that back, to you boy Los."

"Shit he gave it to me. It's yours big brother enjoy it." " Oh yeah and what I was saying about that two hundred and forty four number you said to me if that is the number. That 39 million you got at the second house is gonna get split two ways as soon as we get there."

"What... What up talking about?"

"Okay let me make this as clear as I possibly can. If you sent two hundred and forty four million already, and there's still 39 at the house, Me and You are gonna split that down the middle 19.5 a piece."

"Now do you understanding what I'm saying "

"You serious, man stop play in! " I know you buggin' now..."

"Look at me Big Bruh." "Do I look like I'm playing?" "Shit went smooth down here because of you. "If you want that money wired some place we can do it Thursday night personally."

"Yo... Did you just say if I sent two hundred and forty four tickets and theirs 39 in the house we gonna split it 19.5 a piece."

"Of course I said that."

"Yo Sul, as bad as I wanna keep it all in cash, yes bruh I want you to off shore it for me, but I'm gonna keep the half a ticket (5 hundred grand) with me."

" Okay whatever, but listen. I'm not gonna fly to Atlanta on Thursday, you can bring me in the rig, this way we can move everything at once, and when we leave from down here Thursday morning, we aint never gonna look back at this spot. It's over."

⁙

"Ok Mr. United States Attorney lets go see just what he knows." As they all got up out of their simultaneously headed out of the briefing room it was quick and swift thru that door and down the hall in the direction of the elevator the Assistant United States Attorney made an abundant stop and look dead into the eyes of the now bewildered senor local officer.

"OOh. No.. Sarg. With no disrespect this is how this thing is gonna work. Me and my lead agent are gonna go in the room first, and you're gonna watch us from that one way glass you guys have, because we are gonna put a press on him and bluff him to the point he may want tell us things his mother did illegal when he was a little kid. It works like this because we make the defendants very uncomfortable to which is why our conviction rate is still at 85%. It's just how we work for the 6th Circuit court of Alabama sarg."

He said as he slightly hunched his shoulders in a this is how it is jesture.

"If that's how you guys do things then it's all right with me, I'll just sit back and watch the show from the window." This night, boy I'll tell you has been one roller coaster after another one and I still can't believe that man upstairs is caught up in all this mess." He said as the elevator doors opened and they all entered.

19

"Have you ever seen them or met with any of the people in the pictures personally?" Rasul asked as Carlos then tucked the pics away in his inside pocket of his members only flight jacket. They all shook hands as Los and Sul jumped in a black livery taxi headed back to O'Hara Airport with their next destination of North Carolina in mind to speak with Rasul's uncle Hakeem, they landed in Raleigh about 3 hours later to repeat the process only to find out Uncle Hoc has never met with any of them as well, nor did he ever see the dual in the pictures that his old friend from Florida carried.

"What the hell is going on Nephew? You call me and tell me to stay where I am you'll be here in a few, then you show me some pictures asking me do I know any of these people or have I met with them or they met me now your just like I'm out.

" What the hell" tell me something?"

" Now you know I'm gonna give you the run down, just speeding Unk.. Got a lot on my mind some silly ass dude got caught up by the Alphabet boys a few days ago and are spilling their guys to them and somehow our (BBOP) Organization name has been brought up and now possibly caught up in a drug ring conspiracy in the south somewhere around Alabama. Some dude name Tony V. is yapping his gums like crazy because he's getting ready to have a child and the fact that he just got married a couple week ago doesn't make this thing any better but little does he know I'm gonna be the one to kill him personally the minute the feds let him breath for just that one second slip up. "I will take his last breath after that for sure." Rasul now looked irritated as he paused looking from his uncle to Carlos. "I'm trying to find out if the family ever met any of them or ran across them that's all just in case we gotta clean up some more, feel me."

"Hold up." His uncle said as he reached and grabbed his nephews arm as he was sitting on the passenger side of his black on black BMW X5, because he could clearly see his young one was a little stressed. "Think for a second before you act to fast. Let's get some more details first about this whole situation."

"I got you Unk n I feel you, but if I got to torcher his wife and unborn in front of him I'll find out what, who he knew and exactly everything he spilled his guts about to the government.

"Sul.. Yo! Sul breathe easy I got this you act like it's all about you. I stand to lose more. What you forgot they got one of my main man's Capo and Lieutenant.. I know my main man will stand up strong. "No question", it's his man even though we never met he doesn't realize just what he knows, so let's handle this thing together beloved, we're family first make no mistake about this, he'll be dealt with, no question, but let's get the facts like Unk said first ok. Los said as he now grabbed both his friends arms by the elbows to help clam not just his nerves but Sul's as well.,

"Unk.. We'll holla at you in a few days to keep you posted on what's good Okay"..

Carlos said as he looked at Sul's uncle. " let's get moving Sul we gonna talk a little more on the ride back up top, but Unk stay low right now Sul will hit you up in a few days". Rasul walked away after he hugged him favorite uncle, told him he loved him and gave him the greeting as he then strolled about twenty yards to the small craft, climbing the steps to the jet as Los and Hakeem were closing their talk, he looked back at the two. "Luv you Unk" He said as disappeared into the back of the small plane. Carols said his farewells, then reached into the SUV and hugged Hakeem, then walked away in the direction of the jet, as the old man looked on Los started his climb on the steps then ducked in as the stairs rose up behind and in minutes they were back on the runway ready for take-off as the Golf Stream 200 started making his way down the run way and into the beautiful blue skies. Hakeem look on as the plane disappeared into the clouds as he found himself caught in deep thought about the situation that just transpired between him, his Nephew and his nephews friend and in a silent prayed. "O Allah please look over my nephew, guide him and protect him, please lift that anger from his heart that he's been carrying around for years, I understand what we did was wrong and I'm sure your gonna deal with us one day, but for now please humble that boy just a little 'God willing."

"Listen Los." Sul said with a wild fire look directly at his old friend in eyes.

"Please let me know when either of those dudes get out. If he knows someone from my family, I'll kill him myself. I mean it, Just let me know when he starts running around, I'll handle the rest. I'm just gonna need to be able to get in and out of town on a moment's notice without anyone knowing I was there, "Feel me."

"Any access you need to this baby right here, you got it.. I'll need a few hours for the pilot, that's all, "cool."

"That's cool with me." Rasul said as they headed back to New Jerseys Teterboro airport.

" Now." Let me call my wife and let her know that I'm ok. It's almost 5pm, she'll be getting off work soon. I gotta let her know, I'm gonna pick up the baby from the daycare, then she'll think everything is ok and or wasn't that bad, because if she knew anything about this she'd be stressed all the way out because she's always worrying about me. I love her to death thou.

" Sul, you still scared off Sheema after all these years." He said with a slight chuckle in a playful jester as the Gulfstream was finishing it's decent and headed back towards the Hanger numbered "14." "Sul.. the next time I call you, It'll be because dude made bail.. I can handle it.. "You know that right Sul."

" I'm positive you can Los, I just want to make sure I'm standing over him as he takes his last breath", "You digg".

"You still a Heartless dude Sul".. Carlos was saying as he was standing at the planes doorway while Rasul was getting into his car. Carlos watched him enter his car and drive off the strip to exit the Airport before he was back in the air headed for Miami. "I really need Sul to find out what my guy told the Feds, before Mr. Heartless offs him" I'll talk more about it to him when the time comes, for the showdown, because knowing him he's defiantly gonna make a mess out of that Tony v. dude" were Los's thoughts.20

20

"Now.. as to the other witnesses whom testified thru out this trial did, most of them testified about crimes our clients never contested too. They were past crimes, that they plead guilty to and paid for. He passed on the other hand, we as defense called in witnesses whom testified, that our clients have changed their lives, and lifestyles of crime to being honest productive people of society, giving back to the same communities they once played a part in destroying. They've now helped children, as well as adults, in dealing with gangs, drugs, and violence. They've also given them a place for after school programs, and played mentor to countless youths throughout their cities these past years. Ladies and gentleman, of the jury. The prosecution wants you to believe that Mr. Clif Harper.. The government's star witness is a good and just man. A changed man all of a sudden.. an honest man, who preached every sunday. Who's all of a sudden wants to clear his conscious, from crime and disloyalty to not only his wife and loved one's but his 5 hundred person church congregation, at the same time not go to jail for the crimes that he himself committed and gotten caught up in with his hands in the cookie jar. "He was caught red handed with these two ounces of raw uncut cocaine". He picked them up off of the evidence table, put them down then pointed back towards the table.

"55 kilograms of packed pure cocaine hidden in a secret compart-ment of a vehicle, that was registered to him.

"Him." He pointed to the witness stand. Clif Harper Not any of our clients, but him was charged with 2 counts of transporting and distribution, of cocaine across, not one but 3 different state lines called inner state commerce. Also as you may remember this.. At the time of his arrest, he was caught with an underage stripper, to which he told the local authorities that he thought she was 21 years old, when in fact she was only a 16 year old run away from Atlanta Georgia. This is called statutory rape and endangering the welfare of a minor and sexual assault. A child predator. But the government will look over this because they want the conviction of our clients. How do we explain this part of the trial to our children when they ask you. mom, dad, he's not gonna get in any trouble for that or be put on the child predator register list? No he's not."

"No he won't be. It's ok. We don't want you. meaning him we want them "he had pointed to his clients". She was just a child ladies and gentlemen, she could have been anyone of your children, or mine that this man took advantage of. They also want you to believe that Mr. Harper, "Preacher Man" a.k.a. The Lucky Charm."

"Should be set free because he really didn't mean what he did. It was just a mistake because of hard times. I'm sure you clearly saw that I proved earlier today the fact that not only does he not know any of the defendants with the exception of one, but in fact he doesn't even really know him. "Please turn your attention to the empty wit-ness stand". That Ladies and Gentlemen of the jury, is just what the Government has on our clients, "Nothing." Empty space, trumpet up charges and allegations."

"You've heard lie after clear lie, that the Government's Star wit-ness, who's now in the protection of the United States Marshals for doing whatever Mr. Harper wanted to do. How... Ladies and Gentlemen .. How is he still running around like a free man for getting caught, and our clients on the other hand. Those eight defendants sitting over there, with the fate of their lives in your hands, and their only faults were old news facts that they have prior arrests and convictions. The Star Witness stated, he knew all of the defendants, but he couldn't describe anything outside of what the prosecution cohorts with them. In reality he only thought he knew one of the defendants." He turned from the jury pool towards the defendants table and points."

"He only knows of Mr. Baxtor. and Mr. Baxtors only faults were trusting and believing in a man known to everyone in his home town as a respectable preacher man. They both had dealings with a close and mutual female friend of my client Mr.Baxtor, who girlfriend, died in a fatal car crash, just three weeks after he was released from prison."

"My client was actually the one who informed Mr. Harper of that accident and it was at that point they began speaking about faith and community issues which built a social bond not a friendship as the Star witness described it. Yes Mr. Harper was the one who helped my client Mr. Baxtor with that situation! Now as a determent to you, the jury with an concocted story about the defendant to destroy my clients life."

"Ladies and gentlemen please let us not forget that the star witness Mr. Clif Harper preached the words of God that very same day then ran a mid to upper class dope smuggling operation during his leisure hours of that night he was arrested and every other night before that night for almost 2 years. While his lovely wife, family, and congregation where made to believe he was serving Gods work and word."

21

"How are you doing this morning Mr. Harper? My name is Assistant United States Attorney Michael Kelly, and this is Special Agent Alvin Lewis out of the Miami Dae's F.B.I. Major Crimes Field office. "Would you like a hot cup of coffee, tea or a soda or something?... Are you hungry?..

" Yes please... Do you mind if I ask where Sergeant Thomas is?"

"He's down stairs.. He's still doing some paperwork."

"Now to the matter at hand. Mr. Harper, the Sergeant really likes you, and he really thinks you can help yourself, either a little or a lot it's totally up to you.

Mr. Harper we have you on video dropping off large amounts of cocane to Agent Lewis's partner who's been under cover on this here operation for almost three years now. But do understand this will be your only chance to help yourself. Right now!!"

"I will give you no second chances as of right now the government has taken over this situation that your currently in as well. Listen Mr.

Harper, right now this shit that your caught up in is very deep and if we were to go to the newspapers this morning you'll have no other choice but to resign as the head Pastor of Second Baptist Church because the sex scandal alone especially once we put our twist on it the media will have fields day with this story, But now here's the big but. But… if you come totally clean without any bull shit because right here right now my bull shit antennas are up right now, and just so you understand me I'll bury you so deep your wife won't even wanna come looking for you because of this mess you've made with yourself and your life, but if you give me what I'm sure you know about this morning like I said in that big but this situation won't be as sever I can't guarantee you anything but I have worked with the Judge that will be residing over this case and once I explain just how much you have helped us out along with the other agencies that may want to speak to you about this case in the motion that will be placed before him he normally grants us what we want especially being that you've never been in any trouble before this, plus it's your last and final chance anyway."

"This is a big case and I'm sure there will be more people that will try to help themselves out of their own situations in this case because a lot of people are going to jail for a very long time and I will personally see to that your currently looking at a minimum of twenty years on the drug conspiracy charges and an additional ten for the juvenile down stairs, that's thirty already minimum, plus if you have something downstairs in that jeep that the police towed in here, which I'm sure there will be it will give us not only more solid evidence against you and this case but it may move your thirty year minimum to a life sentence. We already know that your just a mule for the 'Ross Crime Family,' out of Miami". The Assistant United States Attorney held up his hands to stop whatever Mr. Harper was getting ready to tell him something. We don't want you Cliff! We do have you dropping off over one hundred and seventy kilos of un cut rubber sealed manufactured and ready to distribute cocaine over the past three years.

Uh.uh.uh.." The attorney gestured as he shook his head from side to side almost reading Mr. Harpers eyes as they started to tear up and become glassy. Knock,

Knock! Knock!, as three hard thumps came from the other side of the steel door. Agent Alvin Lewis walked over to the door and half opened it as the agent who knocked bend into the door and whispered something into the agents ear. Lewis then turned towards the Assistant United State Attorney looked him dead in the eye then waived him over and as the Attorney got close, the agent then whispered into his ear. "I need to speak to you real quick outside Okay?" The Lead Agent said as he placed his hand into the small of the attorneys back with one hand and with the other hand he grabbed the knob on the door lead him into the hallway Just outside the door. Excuse me for one minute Mr. Harper. The attorney said, then pulled the door closed behind them.

As Mr. Harper watched on, his heart began to race and palpitate because he didn't quite know what was going on but what he did know was that he was in a lot of trouble and might be going to prison for the rest of his life.

"Damn! Damn! Damn! I don't believe what I got myself into. I took that money from my brother-in-law and made a deal with the devil. I not only paid him back but I let that fast money get the best of me and drugs." He shook his head. "Did I really start taking that stuff just to calm my nerves as I took those trips for him then he introduced me to those women who used that junk while they road with me to the drop offs. I really fooled myself into believing I'll b ok because I had God on my side. "Why, Why, didn't I stop once he was pad back?! Why?!" He said as he started banging his fist on the metal table now panting as the tears started to stream down his face, then just as fast he put both hands together and started to pray. "Father God I know what I've been doing was wrong, very wrong, and I know I have to face my consequences but what I'm asking you is to please have some mercy on me and my family, I know this is not just gonna tear my wife and children apart the church, The church is gonna be turned upside down. Lord I didn't know the age of that young just as I know I not only dishonored you but adultery". Just as he really started to go into his prayer, the steel door opened and now it wasn't just the Assistant United States Attorney, and the lead agent there were now two other agents who looked more like octagon kick boxers in there Army fatigue pants and grey hoodies with their Federal ID's hanging from their necks. The whole time the United States Attorney was talking to Preacher man. Sergeant Stan Thomas was watching the screen in front of him from the time they first walked the interview room # 4 with whom he thought was not just a good family friend most off all this man was his Pastor, the man he confided every upset thought into. "Darn this man married me." A community leader sitting across from a top dog in the government's court system. Not trying to believe as he was shaking his head that none of what he was hearing wishing this night was all just one bad dream until he saw one of the agents that Matt brought down to search the SUV in the garage open the interview room door, then rush over to the Lead agent in turn waived the A.U.S.A. outside. sarg. jumped up as well, to meet with them all to find out the latest news on the truck everyone was so concerned about. They both walked out into the hallway on the monitor's screen the was in front of the sergeant, where all the other Agents, plus the now standing local brass. "Mr. Kelly we've just found what looks like 55 kilograms of cocaine in a fake compartment of the vehicle's driving shaft ". All the sargent could do was once again shake his head in even more shock.

"This really can't be happening" he thought he was thinking but said it loud enough for everyone standing to look in his direction.

"Excuse me." The attorney said.

"Excuse me sir. Just thinking out loud."

"Oh okay, no problem." He said to the sarg. then turned. "Thank you Agent Jones..

"Let's go Lead Agent Alvin Lewis said, I think we can break this one real fast! He looks like he's gonna crap his pants any second now"...

"I was thinking the same thing, while we were in there he was so scared right now, any minute he's gonna spill his guts". They both chuckled before they walked back into the Interview #14 with their blank faces on once again. Both men entered, while Pastor Harper was sipping on a steaming hot cup of coffee, with both hands, that one of the officers bought in while the others were in the hallway talking.

" Mr. Harper.. We now have a major problem." The A.U.S.A. said as he placed the several evidence pictures that were just taken just a few moments ago, along with about thirteen other of people, with the exception of his brother in law and a guy name Macky he never saw any of the others before in his life.

"Mr. Harper before I ask you who you may or may not know in these pictures I just placed before you. I need you to understand those Agents behind me standing to your left just found approximately 55 kilo grams of cocaine in that truck you drove in the parking lot of the Ramada Inn were the FBI has you on video surveillance driving into the lot at approximately 7:15 pm with suspect # 2 which she is the young lady down stairs. Mr. Harper with the dope we just found in your SUV just moved you up the scale to a life sentence, no matter if this is your first time or not being locked up."

"What do you mean life."

"Life... Life. Cliff like you'll never see your family in the free world again, if you don't start talking.. "I mean RIGHT NOW!" The A.U.S.A. half shouted as he banged on the desk.

"Do you understand, what's going on here!" "We have proof you've brought several vehicles in your name that are directly linked to the 'Ross Crime Family'. These vehicles have been transporting cocaine throughout the Southern States."

"Mr.Harper you was caught, just hours ago having sex with a minor, and she's admitted to having sex with you for some time now, that means on more than one occasion. This spells out big trouble, for you!"

"What can I do to help myself ?"

"Now you get the Picture."

"Would you like anything else to drink?" I'm not asking you this because you look a little restless because for the next few hours myself and Mr. Lewis have a lot of questions on our minds and we're wondering if you may be of some benefit not just to us but mostly to yourself because as you can see Mr. Harper you are caught up in a major drug trafficking ring and depending on the information you may or may not have for us it cannot just determine your freedom, it can also determine whether or not you'll get a bail because right now you're looking at a life sentence not because of the drugs that where found today but the conspiracy that you have been a part of over the last several months to which in fact almost thirteen months total". Now Mr. Harper right now you're in some deep shit point blank period. Meaning if we go to the newspapers this morning you'll not only have to resign as a pastor of the Second Baptist Church because the sex scandal alone will have your followers in an up roar especially once we put our own twist on things, but now here's a big but. But you can come totally clean without any bull shit and just know that my bullshit antennas are up right now, I'll bury you so deep your wife won't even coming looking for you and if she does it'll be because she wants you to sign some divorce papers because of this mess you've help to create. Now I'm back to that big but that I was just talking about. But if you help yourself and give me what I'm sure you know this can all be swapped under the rug for the most part for now. We'll call the judge and because you have no prior criminal history we'll let him know that we're pushing these charges back until you finish helping us in this investigation. I can't promise what will happen at the end of this case because it's up to the judge. You'll go home sometime this morning to your wife and children, doing things as you normally do. If you can provide what we ask of you, you will be set up with Mr. Lewis here to which he no everything going on in your life especially your dealing because as of right now no one knows we have you and what we have you for. With the exception of the hotel manager but we can fix that as well. Mr Harper I'm giving you an opportunity of your life time and this will be your only opportunity to save yourself because once we start rounding up your codefendants for this case you can best believe whomever knows you have anything to do with this there gonna cut a deal with us and give you up because of who are in this town. Your currently looking at twenty years for these drugs we have today and an additional ten years for the juvenile that's coming down from her high sitting in a cell down stairs. That's thirty total and we're just starting an at your age it's a death sentence because you'll never see the outside world again after the court proceedings are over". "Now for starters, if you help us, we will help you as much as we can. We can possibly get you a bail for those 55 kilo's (OR Bail a.k.a. own recognizance bail) meaning a release on your own recognize bail, and keep this thing hush, hush for as long as we can, you know what I mean". But we may need you to work ever further for us on the outside once your free. we'll talk to the judge about bail for everything asap, but this all depends on how truthful you are with us, right here, right now! But if you lie to us about anything we ask you because we know things, if you lie to us the deals off, and I'll make sure your plea deal is at least three hundred and sixty months, plus we'll see that the Judge doesn't give you a bail, because you are a flight risk, and a danger to the community, because you'll be known as a sexual predator having sex with a minor. Please understand me. If I walk out those doors". He pointed to the door across the room, but as he was putting his arm back on the table the now defendant lightly grabbed it. But as he did the agents rushed hushed towards him he then put both hands in the air in and said. "Please stop."

"I was just trying to get his attention". " I.. I'll tell you whatever you want to know.."

"Please.. please… let me help myself ". This would never be happening if only I would've just asked church for the money. Instead of going to my brother in law for help. I.. I.. got greedy. Dear God, I'm sorry, please believe me. That young lady that was with me tonight. She was just supposed to come along for the ride as always, to which we started having fun, one thing lead to another after making the drop off safe, with the sex and recreational drug use, because she would always tell me she was horney." The United States Attorney stopped him.

"What else can you tell me?... Do you know any of those people in these photos."

23

February 13th 2002; The last meeting of the family.

It was almost 7am in the morning while a light mist of rain fell as the Gulf Stream G4Lear jet landed on the runway of Teteboro's private air strip.

As the plane headed for hanger #4, a black limo van pulled up beside the hanger, waiting for the door of the plane to depressurize, then open. Once the door started to descend the driver of the van walked up into the plane, two minutes later he emerged from the plane with two large suitcases, then loaded them into the back of the van, then went back into the jet for yet another trip. He repeated the cycle once more, until he exited on the third trip with a wheel-chair. He placed it at the bottom of the stairs. A couple of seconds later, 3 people exited the plane, the last occupant was helped down the stairs by the other two occupants into his wheelchair. Then into the front seat of the van as the driver then loaded the chair into the back of the vehicle. Pulling away from the hanger the driver punched a few numbers into his phone then gave the time of pick up then placed the phone back into the inside of his jacket pocket as he headed thru the terminal exit, then made a right turn onto Teteboro Road, headed north towards the interstate route 46 east intersection which was about a quarter of a mile from the small air strip. The driver made a left hand turn onto the expressway east-bound. Ten minutes later the van was pulling up into the upper level's toll plaza, of the George Washington Bridge. As they were midway across the bridge, the front seat passenger looked up at the welcome to New York, home of the empiror state banner billowing in the wind and misty rain. The vehicle made the right hand turn off of the bridges first exit then rounded the off ramp, to enter onto the Henry Hudson Parkway's North/South ramp. Taking the southbound exit under the overpass headed down the Hudson River Parkway, until they reached the 93rd street exit. Rounding another overpass alongside the river, then kept going straight down 93rd now headed south towards 5th Avenue. The rain now starting to come down as the van past thru Central Park with the wind shield wipers moving like there on turbo as the driver sped thru a yellow traffic light, then made a quick left into an underground garage parking lot of a building on the corner of 93rd Street and 5th Avenue, by passing all the parking spaces. The van drove directly up to the garages elevator. The driver walked around to the back of the van to retrieve the wheel chair then to the door of the front passenger to help him out of the van, while the other two occupants quickly and swiftly made their way grabbing their own luggage. The driver pushed the chair up to the elevator then went to retrieve his luggage as one of the other two men pushed the button for the elevator. The driver then pulled a key card out of his wallet as the door opened and pushed it into a slot below the (PH) button then pushed that button. The elevator hoisted the four men up towards the top floor. As it rose upwards the driver of the van picked up the elevators phone. Pressed a couple numbers, then announced the arrival of the other three occupants into the phone. The door opened into the back of the penthouse's dining room, as the driver started to lift the safety gate, five other men, whom were all in the living room turned in their chairs simultaneously as the meeting of the brother hood was about to begin.

"Yes.. only three.. I think this one's name is Lucious Banana.. I'm not sure but I think that's his name. but I'm really not sure if that's his last name. From my understanding he's one mean dude with a lot of money, they say he once killed a whole family in Madison Georgia, because the husband tried to run off with his money after he the husband who was a mechanic was supposed to put a few stash spots into some of Lucious's vehicles. Then borrowed some money from banana because of a gambling problem realized he couldn't pay back the money he rigged one of Lucious's main cars so if he went over fifty miles an hour and tried to stop his breaks would fail, turns out Lucious crashed ad broke his neck. Once he started walking again he assassinated the whole family n made the man watch, then he turned around and cut both the man's hands off before he killed him as well they found the mans on the desk in his repair shop. This guy's name is Big Mike". He pointed to another photo. "He's my brother in law, my wife's little brother, used to stay in trouble, but always had a little money that's why."

"He's the one who sends the girl with me and gave me the money I needed before I got greedy, plus he paid for all the vehicles that he told me I had to put in my name because if the police ran the plates it would come back to a pastor and they wouldn't suspect anything, with the exception of my car and my wife's car. A couple years ago my brother in law told me that he'd come into a lot of money if I needed anything to let him know, he wouldn't say anything around my wife and the operation that he's doing is simple. No one knows what's going on, so when my situation came about, I called him and asked him can he help me out of a situation. He came to my house we talked he said he'd help about an hour later he came back with what I asked for, and I told him if he ever needed me for anything to just call. Low and behold he called me about a month later and asked me if I can drop off a car by one of his friend's house n just leave the keys under the driver's seat. I agreed to do it without question, he then told me to call him once I was there so I did, when I was about to get out of the car my brother in law told me on the phone he'd had something for me in the clove compartment. I called him right back because I thought it was a mistake, he told me."

"That's all you Big bruh" "Then his phone disconnected. I got extremely nerves because of the money, but I let the devil start talking to me telling me to keep it, so I had to keep telling myself I didn't do anything wrong to justify my actions. Almost a week later he called me again and asked me if I could drop off another vehicle, this time it was a little farther but someone would ride with me, which was with me tonight and, is the girl down stairs right now. My brother in law then told me with the exception of the person who picks up the vehicle and drops it off. No knows when its coming or going. It's a sweet lick and I'll give you two grand a week if you could do this for me, meaning him." He said as long as I follow everything he says to do and never ask any questions about the vehicles or what's in them. Just drive by the rules. A couple times I saw duffle bags all the way in the back of the SUV's and asked what was in them and all he would tell me was to never mind them and never open them because the drop off would know and someone would be in real trouble feel me!" so I never looked even in the back anymore, I just prayed every time before I got in those vehicles. "This guy right there.. He pointed to a picture neither the A.U.S.A or any of the agents were expecting him to no.

"What guy." Said the Attorney "That guy right there! His name is Hamid.. Hamid Baxtor. He owns the car dealership where I bought the vehicles from, he always gave us great deals.

"What do u mean by he?. Like He, his car lot or He, himself?"

"Hamid, himself. We used to talk a lot a few years back, then I stopped seeing him then I started hearing the rumors."

"What rumors?" said the Lead Agent as he looked from the A.U.S.A. back towards the other agents then back at the man known as Preacher man.

"Just rumors.. They say he hooked up with some people from New York, who have a lot of money.. 'You know Kingpins'.. I do know that Hamid sold so drugs before he when to prison because he'd told me that personally. I'd recken you guys already know this." The lead Agent cut him short. "Go on Mr. Harper."

"Anyways, they say them New York boys was down here, the all of a sudden two of the biggest drug dealers in Birmingham were found dead in their cars with bullets in their heads, Now they say Hamid filthy rich. He owns three car lots, a clothing store in Fairfield, plus he is a partner in Ms. Sadie's Group home right across the street from here.. Oh yeah.. He has a community center for the kids in his town, Hobson city. He's also partners with this organization called the B.B.O.P." "Black Brothers of Promise."

"Do you know any of his partners?" would u know their faces if you see them?"

"All I really know is Hamid. He told me one day that he was saving all his money from his hustling days, and built his empire with it. He also told me that his partners were also ex-felons, who've changed their lives as well."

"Mr. Harper.. just tell me out right! Do you think that this Baxtor guy still has dealings in the streets?" Agent Lewis said with a very stern voice and look on his face.

"I don't know."

"Mr. Harper if we find out your holding back on us I'll personally bury you."

"Hold on Agent Lewis I don't think Mr. Harper will lie to us or hold anything back from us, not even one person at this point, right Mr. Harper?"

"Yes Mr. Kelly I won't lie to you, or to you Agent Lewis, as God is my witness. "I really don't know, but I'll try my best to find out whatever I can, if you want me too."

"Maybe.. what else do you know." Mr. Harper went on for several hours talking to the government. He also made at least several recorded phone calls to the drop spots he was supposed made it to the day before,. He even called his brother in law to get him on a wiretap.

All in all Pastor Clif Harper was given a bail the very same morning, and released to help work with the government, now as an informant. It was like last night never existed, because the government hid the arrest and placed a gag order on the whole police station, so it was to never be mentioned by anyone in the local police department.

"Why." because the government can do what it wants to do and never have to answer to anyone.

They make the rules. But what the government didn't know was that someone in that local police station worked for the 'Ross Crime Family'.

That same night after meeting with Carlos, Rasul had called an emergency meeting with the team he was running with before this big dream, run. This circle, very small but very dangerous. They all grew up in a small projects they called Sugar Hill these were old loyal friends that made their own way and their own money. As he pulled his Red Range Rover into the front projects, he half smiled watching a couple of his lifelong friends in front of the building shooting dice. As he pulled in, he heard a very familiar voice that yell from the crowd.

"Yo Pugg.. Park that shit right there my dude." He pointed to a space right next to his Minnie van.

It was one of those child hood friends you can call a real brother because they been thru everything with you, and would never turn his back on you, he just had one problem and that was gambling it was always something especially if he was losing and I could tell at this moment that's what was going on.

"Twone, what's good my dude, aint been over here in a minute. But I see you just won't stop." Rasul said as he started to get out of his truck then remembered he'd had his 40 caliber on his hip, He grabbed it, then reached back into the suv and placed it in the arm rest then shut the door behind him, the headed for the dice game.

"This what I do." Antwone said as they both shook hands and hugged each other.

"Where Cee at?"

"He sitting right there in his car." Twone said as he pointed to a white 750i BMW parked almost on the side of the building that they were standing at, three of the doors opened on that car as he pointed. Three men emerged, the driver was Sul's little brother Cee, who stood about 5'8" light skin baldhead and of medium built, he had sharp features with a sometimes full shadow beard, kept a 357 magnum snug on his hip like a belt. And Dee who stood about the same height and weight, but was brown skinned, full beard with short waived hair. He kept a 44 desert eagle on him all the time as well. They were known in the projects as two guns. They pretty much got their own money, but when it came to putting in work, they were known all over the city. Now D-nice on the other hand also moved on his own. Quiet dude, but a gun specialist. The Feds tried to snatch him up for running guns up from the south, but when it was time for his trial the informants ended up missing so they had to cut him loose.

"Damn Rudie, what took you so long to get here?" Cee said to Rasul as they were making their way to him. These were Sul's ace in the whole because regardless what was going on, whatever he told these three or did with the trio stayed within them.

"My wife was tripping because early this morning, my man called me from Miami, told her it was very important that he speak to me, and because I told her I had to go see what he was talking about, she became a nerves rec. I chilled with her when I got back from meeting dude n told her I'll be back in a little while, so now I'm here." He said as they all embraced him. "Let's go in the building so we can talk." They walked into the building, then took the elevator to the 9th floor apartment 9B. That was a three bedroom apartment where all of them would chill at any time because they all had keys to it. It was what they called their safe house.

"Rudie what's really good bruh?" you aint been over on this side in a minute".   D-Nice said.

"I know I've been busy with the kids in my program, but now I need a couple eyes and a couple hands." The Feds trapped some dudes off in the south and a couple of them are talking to much feel me. I'm going down there in a few days, because I need to bury these dudes. I'll have the address on them hopefully by tomorrow morning. D I need you to holla at your peoples in south, and let them know we need some throw away heat (guns). May need a couple of silencers for them as well."

"You got that bruh, I'm on it right now." D-Nice pulled his Star Tec cell phone out his pocket, hit a couple buttons, then walked towards the living room couch as he started talking into his phone.

"Listen, dude who called me this morning it tied into everything but I wanna handle this one personally, I'm glad you guy's cleaned up my situation after my run, but this has to happen asap."

"I got twenty five grand on each head. I need you both because I'm not sure what I'm going down there against, but before we do what we do, we need to know what they told the Fed's. we all gotta be on the same page about this because I need to know everything before they die."

"You got that." They both said at the same time.

"When we rollin'?" Cee said.

"As soon as I find out where their resting their heads at night for sleep, My man from Florida said he'll fly us where ever but I don't even want him to know when we make this move just in case, something go's wrong feel me."

"Yeah I feel better the way we move anyway." Dee said.

"On another note what's going on with you guys?" I miss coming around here, but you know how it is when I said I was done I'm done. I just have to see this right here through."

"We good, me and Dee about done with the streets as well we was talking about it while we were sitting in the car waiting for you. I'm proud of you big bruh you walked away and you doing real good, I'm getting sick of this shit personally. Same shit day in day out, I've been looking at buying a few trucks and starting my own company, in a few months."

"Damn, lill bruh I've been waiting a long time to here this." Rasul backed away from the table and hugged his little brother, then he hugged his other brother Dee.

"listen I'm gonna get out of here, before the wife start looking for me, lol I'm gonna hit the both of you in the am." He walked over to where D-nice was still on the phone engaged in a conversation. "Yo Dee.. I'm out I'll holla at you in the am ok."

"Okay. bet." They embraced the Sul headed out the door down the stairs and out the front door of the propjets to where they were still playing dice.

"Damn you gone already Pugg?"

"Gotta go I'll be back up this way tomorrow."

"Mannn.. Stop lying pugg you know you ain't coming back up here tomorrow."

"By Allah, I'll be back tomorrow InshaAllah."

"What?"

"God Willing, beloved." Rasul said as he jumped into his truck.

24

"Mr. Harper the star witness testified under oath that he did in fact preach during the day, then turn around and play the Devil's advocate at night.. He also testified to the use of narcotics.. He testified to having extra marital affairs on his wife of more than twenty five plus years. He swore for better and or for worse, thru sickness and in health, and till death do us apart, and those were vow's he made with God, but choose to break then because of greed. Now, let's not forget the sixteen year old little girl, he was caught with at the time of his arrest, that the government just swept under the rug until these court proceedings and even then, He testified to sleeping with her multiple times. Please remember, when he first got caught, he made a statement to the local police that the girl was 21 years old, and he never slept with her, but that one time. He lied about that."

"Also something to remember… When the now19 year old female took the stand a few days ago, she said she'd been sleeping with Preacher Man for almost 3 years before the arrest, and last but not least.. He testified to laundering drug proceeds through the 6th Avenue Baptist Church of Worship, where he resided as Pastor for almost twenty nine years." One of God's Temples. He looked directly at juror #3. he lead counsel for the "B.B.O.P. Organization." Walked over to the witness stand, and picked the Bible up off the wide rail, that the Preacher Man had sworn upon for the past couple of days during his testimony. He then sat the Holy book on the guardrail of the jury box right in front of juror #3. Bent down to the point they were almost at eye level and asked the question. " If not this book… Who can We trust."

Rrriiinnng, rrriiinnngg, rrriiiinnnngggg. "Damn why my big bruh calling me so early in the morning." "Hello."

"Peace lill bro I know it's like 7:30 but we need to make this move. I just called Dee.

"I'm gonna scoop him up then I'm coming to get you ok." Imma call D-Nice once I get off the phone with you". Aiight I should be ready by the time you pick Dee up an come get me, I'll see you in a minute."

"Okay, Okay cool peace lill bro see you then." Both lines disconnected. Sul's phone started to cherp. "Hello."

"Sul.. It's me Los.. I faxed you those three address and that safe house address to that # you gave me. What's the plan you need me up there."

"Chill my friend Imma go pick that up around noon today, but I'll hit you sometime tonight n let you know what's good ok?"

"Okay Sul I know you got this." But what Carlos didn't know was the plan was already being put in motion.

"You already no beloved, I'll call you later." They disconnected. Sul pushed another set of numbers in his phone, and as it started to ring he was now in Jersey pulling up to his pops house, as he beeped his horn twice, the line on the other end of the phone picked up. "Twone what's good you still at the gym?"

"Yeah why what's up?"

"I need to use your van for a couple days.. I'm bringing you my Mercedes right now ok."

"What.. what you need my shit it for?"

"Mann.. stop asking so many questions, damn you nosy as hell."

"What…. How the hell you calling me noisy? That's my shit!"

"Listen I'm trying to do something, and I need a different vehicle. It ain't like I'm gonna use it to do anything crazy. Anything happens to it. My word, you can have my joint, need I say more?"

"Naw.. come get it, how long you gonna be?"

"I'll be there in like 5 minutes peace." Sul hung up the phone before any more questions came about. "Sup lill bruh?" He said to his younger brother as he jumped into the car.

"What's up?" Where Cee at?.."

"We gonna get him now. First I gotta stop down the street at the gym so we can pick up Antwon's van, more room feel me."

"O okay I'm sure that nigga asked you a lot of questions, you no he noisy as hell."

"You no he did." They both laughed while Sul parked his car next to the van, where he was already waiting outside for him.

142

"Yo pug where you going, I see you got Dee with you."

"Twon I gotta take care of something I'll be back either tonight or tomorrow ok damn bruh." They exchanged keys, and he quickly jumped on the interstate. ten minutes later they were pulling into Cee's underground garage, to which he was already walking towards the van.

"Damn Rudie I know, Twon asked you a millon questions."

"That's what I said.. even when we pulled up he was asking Rudie questions."

All three of them laughed as they headed for the New Jersey Turnpike South. Their first stop was at the Maryland house where they gassed up, then grabbed something to eat. They stopped a couple more times but 13 hours later, they pulled into a little motor lodge just outside of Madison, Georgia.

"Listen.. we gonna get a couple hours rest then case where the address are at. Real talk I wanna tryna kill these dudes tonight, no one knows where down here and no one knows their home yet, it's the best time to move, Feel me. then we can drive to my mother's house."

"Yo.. Rudie. you aint tired? you just drove like 15 hours."

"Of course.. Cee. That's why I said we can get a few hours rest, plus I know ya'll ready to smoke."

"Hell yeah.. you already no.. it's good for the soul."

25

Ladies and gentlemen of the jury. Mr. Harper a.k.a. Preacher man, not only swore in under oath yesterday. He swore into oath over twenty plus years ago,, that he'd love and protect with due honesty under a covenant of guardianship as a god fearing man of the cloth. To be guide and leader, for the people of his church and this book. (He pointed to the Bible that was still sitting on the guardrail in front of juror #3). That same book he put his right hand on two days ago and again today". Counsel now picked up the book. "This same book Mr. Clif Harper used as a deception Point!

Then hid behind the words of this book, and deceived everyone that believed in his calling as a good and just man. What I am trying to point out to you, Ladies and gentlemen of the jury is that, if he could make. "No strike that." Bold face lies. To his family, his friends, and congregation, for almost thirty years. So now I ask you. Why in the world would he now tell the truth to all of you these past few days." He looks from one juror to the next juror. Seeing the curiosity in some of their faces especially Juror #2 Now readjusting his tie, once more with both hands, then took a second look at the jury, then he looked across at the A.U.S.A. Michael Kelly and his staff, then he looked at all the defendants, one slow look at a time, and lastly turning half circle to face the Judge…..

"We rest our case."

＊

"Cee.. Chestnut street right! What's the house address, 32 right?" Sul said as he looked back at him from the front passenger seat.

"Yeah, I think it's that yellow and white house second from the corner."

"Ok.." Dee pull around the corner and park right there, but first circle this block I wanna see whats going on,". He pointed just around the corner, while putting on his favorite black leather riding gloves. "Keep the van running Dee, I'm gonna get out right, Imma walk back to the van ok." He jumped out the van with the 40 caliber, pulled his hoodie over his head, then started walked around the back of the house.

"If he's in there, imma come get you."

"Aiight, you know I'm ready."

"Cool." Just as Sul neared the back of the house he became excited and his heart started racing because he just saw the guy from the picture in his front pocket sitting in the living room watching television in just his underwear. He lightly stepped on the back porch because he didn't see any motion detectors, then tried the door knob. His heart really started to race when he turned the knob and the door opened. "Damn Cee gonna have to miss this one because I might not have a second chance." Pulling the silencer out of his front pocket, and screwed it on, as he put his phone in his sock just in case anything went wrong. It was Rasul slowly opened the back door, for his size it was almost unbelievable how he moved like a cat, and this was one of those moments, as he entered thru the kitchen, he couldn't believe what was going on right now especially with the gun pointed straight ahead as he was entering the living, if Craig G looks to his left right now at least he might have the chance to duck, yell, and or at least tried to run, but he doesn't, and by the time he does look the first bullet is in his brain, while the second one was tearing thru his heart. The bullets sounded like someone just spit on the floor twice. Crage G could do nothing but hold his heart and stirred at Sul as he approached him pulling a hook knife from his belt buckle not knowing what was coming next, especially when blood was running down his face, and he couldn't figure out why words couldn't come out of his mouth as he was now coughing up. "I'll be the last face you'll ever see again. Sul said as he stepped behind Crage G and put the hook knife to his through, and quickly snacked G's atoms apple out. Grabbed a blanket off the couch, whipped the blad, then wrapped Crage G in the chair he was sitting in as if he was asleep and walked right out the back door. Took him all but 6 minutes and 27 seconds to be exact, as he looked at his watch closing the door. Pulled his phone out of his sock, then walked back around the house towards the van. "Move over Cee. Dee pull off." Sul said as he opened the side sliding door jumping into the second row seat next to his brother.

"Damn Rudie what's good?" What took so long?" You think he in there?"

"Dee.. make this left off Dixie highway, then another left at the second light. That should be West Jefferson Street, then a right, let's see where that safe house is. Oh yeah bruh, he was in there alright. One down, two to go."

"Damn nat was matrix shit if you hit him that fast."

"Naw, I was walking around the house dude was watching tv drunk in his underwear, and forgot to lock his back door. He won't make it to court"! "Dee make this quick right." Sul said, as he was looking at the papers he pulled out of his right front pocket.

"We should only be about five minutes away." "This friggen Tony V dude told because of his pregnant wife. He better hope she not there."

"Fuc you talking about Rudie."

"She gon have that baby tonight, that's what I'm talking about!" If he didn't care why should I!"

"What you mean?? You talking like you cut the baby out or something?" Cee said looking at his brother. "Yo you trippen bruh."

"Naw bruh he tripped, I'm just picking up the pieces." "This dude got the nerve to be staying at this Budget Inn right here on Eatonton road." Sul said as he shook his head.

"Pull over Dee, don't shut it off, come on Cee lets walk around this place first, shit crazy, ain't but two cars out here. He on the second floor, room 203."

"Only good thing, it's by the stairs and the ice machine, I only seen one camera and that was by the front neon signs in and out door. Damn, why they got him here?" This ain't no safe house."

"He wanted to spend a couple days here, then he's supposed to be moved on Monday morning."

"They ain't got no agents watching him?"

" I don't really know, my contact didn't say anything about anyone sitting on him unless they have one in the room with him, which I'm sure we would have been warred about prior to this ride because my contact is very through".

"Don't nobody know he home yet right?"

"No, but I'm sure the boys ain't to far so keep your eyes open. Listen, If it don't feel right we can go back to the van and re-plan this aiight."

"Aiight.. But you know what? "Mann.. let me just knock on the door, and ask him something stupid. If he answers and it looks like I gotta clean shot, imma hit him in his head and we out." If someone else answers then we'll re think this. Bet?"

"Okay cool." Sul said to his lill brother Cee. Whom was now stripped down to a white tee-shirt to pose as a hotel guest looking for a light for his cigarette.

Rasul watched from the bottom steps half watching the parking lots parameter as his brother thumped three times on the door. A couple seconds later the door opened slow, and within seconds, he saw three flashes from his brothers gun as he watched him enter the room. A minute or two later he was out the room headed down the steps. "Damn bruh...You aint waste no time. What if someone else was in there and started yelling, that shit could've drawn a lot of attention."

"Damn Rudie you act like this was my first time. I could see when dude opened the door no one was in their unless they were in the bathroom, that's why I went in.."

"As I walked out I hit him two more times in the head to make sure he wasn't getting' back up."

"Aiight I'll meet you in the van let me run back in the room I gotta check something out.. only be two minutes." Sul jogs up the steps and quickly walked into the room. A little over Three minutes later he exited the room with what looked like a stuffed pillow case.

"Okay lets go" Rasul said as he rolled the side door back on the van an jumped into the back seat. "Yo I need you to stop at that quick stop we passed when we first got off the highway I need some ice and a cooler."

"Yo Rudie, what the hell is dat?"

"What?"

"Come on bruh, you know what I'm talking about. As a matter of fact, I don't even wanna know."

"Good," Rasul said then half chuckled.

"Dis nig crazy," the driver of the vehicle shot back. "Yo just tell us one thing?"

"Please tell us we ain't gonna ride around with whatever's in that damn sack?"

"Oh hell no. We gon drop this off on dudes mothers porch then head to Alabama to holla at that last dude. I'm gonna enjoy killing his ass."

"Big bruh no disrespect but you're a certified nut, you ain't tired.. it seems like we ain't been to sleep in two days."

"I'm good my adrenalin is going because my freedom might depend on this ish. I'll drive once we drop this off Aiight? So y'all can get some rest."

"Okay cool."

"Dis gotta all happen before morning because once this hits the news, all hell is gonna break loose and them alphabet boys are gonna bug all the way out, and be all over the place at the same damn time."

"THE TAKE DOWN"

"THE FINAL CHAPTER"

"Brothers, seven years ago we walked into this thing, "Called my dream." "Our Dream." To have everything we need to keep us from ever getting into any more trouble, and or going back to prison. We formed our Brother hood B.B.O.P. It has risen to a height that very few whom came home from prison an accomplished. Tasks such as the one's we have. We've cleaned up our neighborhoods and gave our children and young adults something to do besides getting high, skipping school, and hanging on the street corners, We've given a lot of the children in our communities a place to escape them streets with after school programs and just a change of life for them, and that's been real because it was so much fun."

"Damn where we at?" Dee said as he looked over at his big brother driving.

"I should be at this old dudes house in about 15 minutes according to these directions."

"Man we in Alabama already? What you was doing a hundred miles an hour?"

"Not really but at times I was pushing it a little, shit the sun you'll be coming up in a few hours, I need this ish done, feel me."

"Yeah I feel you. Yo' Cee knocked out back there."

Sul looked in the rear view mirror at his younger brother, and with a silent prayer hoped one day this would be behind all of them. "Yeah he dead right now."

They drove in silence, Sul looked over at Dee through the corner of his eyes to see if Dee was now sleep as well, but he wasn't I guess he was in his own thoughts as well. This old dude didn't live in city limits he lived out in the country so this should be like taking candy from a baby were his thought as he pulled off the side off the road at a nice little distance of the old man's house. He looked in the back, Cee was still sleep.

He put the van in park then killed the lights.

"Dee we gonna leave him sleep I don't need you to come I just need you to stand outside this thing just in case I do need you, or you hear something coming my way okay."

"Got you bro."

As he got out of the van he put his gloves on, the half mask, then pulled his huddie over his head the entered the lightly wooded area with an old set of railroad tracks that ran behind the house. As he crossed over the tracks he stepped on a small branch that made what sounded like a loud crackle in the quiet hours of the morning. Now standing in total silence, to see if he now hears anything, moments later... Nothing.

"Good no dogs." He whispered to himself, as his adrenalin started to rush now.

"This should be really easy," and to add to it the back door wasn't even lock, as he tried the knob and as quietly as he could, pushed the door into the kitchen, then slowly entered looking around at every inch of what he could see, now all the way into the kitchen his eyes adjusted as he now saw a faint light in the hall way to the living room, the master bedroom where the old guy slept was the last door passed the hallway bathroom according to the directions n layout. Now half-way thru the house Past the steps was another door that was half opened with its light on and what sounded like either a tv very low or someone whispering, with his right hand he pulled his gun from the back of his waist band.

"Damn, I hope I ain't gotta do whomever is in that room first," because the carpet was so thick he was able to move very quick to that room as he looked in, he thought he struck gold as he saw the old man just in front of him kneeling leaning forward with something in his hands.

"Turn around and if you attempt to make a noise imma kill you and everybody in this bitch." The old man jumped so hard Sul almost shot him, but hesitated because he really wanted to look this guy in the eye.

"Please don't do this." He said as he turned his body around on his knees. He now looked up at Sul. "Please young man.. Please don't do this. My whole family is in this house. Please young man don't do this.. We all make mistakes, I've been asking God since I got caught up in this mess, to please see me thru this.. The Feds told me there was a great chance that my life was in danger, and I told them God will protect me from everything, he knows my heart." Sul inched a little closer to him with the barrow of the silencer to his head then whispered.

"Shhhh." You make one more sound, you gonna be the reason everybody in this house will dies." But as he was whispering this to the old man he looked down an realized the man was holding a bible in his hands, then in a quick glance of the small room he took a deep breath, then asked. "What are you."

"I'm a pastor young man."

"Stop talking so loud. I'm not gonna tell anymore."

"Please listen to me, or at least let me pray before you do this, to make my last peace with God." With tears in his eyes he said then looked down at his bible an started to pray. By the time he stopped praying an looked up the Big man in all black with the mask wasn't there anymore. The pastor slowly rose to his feet, and out the room.

Looking back and forth down the hall, the door to the bed room was still closed the way he left it, his only choice was to see if the masked man was in the kitchen, as he walked in there he looked at the back door then out into the shallow wooded area in his back yard. Was this just a dream as his heart was still beating fast, he looked back down at the book in his hand as it was already shaking, then looked up out the window at the sky, and whispered "Thank you.

"Rasul, hold up.. Hold up one second, big bruh.. before you finish." Taheed said, as he stood up with a big grin on his face and both hands midway above his chest as in a stop gesture. "I just want every-one to know. Me and my girl.. naw my better half Gena, eloped, this past weekend.. Where now a real married couple." He stated as he looked around the table at his brothers, whom were now just as happy as he was, with the exception of Rasul, who had a look on his face, with worry in his eyes. As the congratulations went around the table, the talking about the celebrations and the how's and when of the reception will take place, as the brothers shook his hand.

"Shit." Sul said to himself, as he sat back in his chair looking at all the happy faces, then talking more to himself, than ever one else. " Damn.. I wish this situation could be put off, but it can't." he said as he had his head in his hands.

"What.. Damn.. Sul what's good? You ain't happy for me.. you the one always preaching about marriage." He looked up, placed both his hands on the table, then stood up as now everyone was looking at him.

"Excuse me everyone! I am so sorry to be the bearer of bad news of this precious moment, because I feel like the grim reaper saying this, in spite of what I just heard."

"Gentlemen.. We have a serious dilemma and problem on our hands." He reached down on near the side of his leather sofa chair, and picked his briefcase up. Placed it on the mahogany oak stained conference table, then pulled out a short stack of legal size envelops. "Please take one, then pass the rest around the table." As they did what he asked, each person started to tear at them. Siraj being the first one to open his.

"Yo.. What the hell is this? Are you serious.. Or is this shit a joke?" Now everyone was looking at each other, then all the attention turned to the one, who called this meeting, Rasul.

"What the hell is this, Sul... "This why you called this meeting?. Let me guess the government trumped up charges against us."

"Big Bruh.. You know me.. I wish I can say this was a joke. But it's not. It's very far from one. Plus I will never play with anyone this way.

My connect from Miami, had one of his sources send me this yesterday afternoon. Los even flew up here to talk to me face to face, Last night. Him and a few of his men are facing the same type of charges, with the exception of four felony murders charges, and the United States Attorney for the 6th Circuit Court, State of Florida was going after the death penalty."

"I think Carlos has left the states as of this morning. I've been trying to contact him all morning, even before any of you got here, I've been pushing speed dial on his number up until this point, with no luck. So we now know what we're facing. Each one of them were slowly reading over the contents in disbelief. "Damn I've done a lot of crazy ish in my life and with everything I tried to justify It in my head, but just couldn't shoot no Pastor, we all have our wrongs but not someone who's anointed by God, he wasn't no street dude that we normally dealt with that dude is a real Pastor, I don't know what the hell he was thinking about when he got caught up, but I really hope he does the right thing."

UNITED STATES OF AMERICA
DISTRICT COURT OF ALABAMA

UNITED STATES OF AMERICA

Vs

THE B.B.O.P. ORGANIZATION
Naming Eight defendants) INDICTMENT # 97-104-02
)
SHABAZZ YOUNG) Conspiracy; To Manufacturing
SIRAJ YOUNG) and the Distribution of 10,000
RASUL YOUNG) Kilograms or more of Cocaine
ASHARI YOUNG) Under the R.I.C.O. law from
ESA YOUNG)
HAMID BAXTOR)
TAHEED SHAKUR)

INDICTMENT OF ALL PARTIES

Re: Honorable Judge Billy H. Walls, Office of the Clerk
    United States District Court 7th Circuit
    Northern District of Alabama
    Hugo L. Black United States Courthouse
    1729-5th Avenue North
    Birmingham, Alabama 35203-2040

Date: February 13, 2002

Your Honorable Judge Billy H. Walls, I am respectfully re-
questing warrant arrests for the following eight names listed
above, on matters of violent narcotics trafficking, and the ap-
prehension of these individuals immediately. Please see page
two through six on these matters.

"Sul.. I know this ain't no sick joke or anything, but where the hell did all this shit come from. I thought we had all the bases covered?"

"We did and we still do! These people have no one to place us anywhere. "We just have to see how this damn thing plays out"! Rasul looked out at each and every one of his family members. His eyes started to fill with salted water, but these tears were tears of rage, and sorrow for his family, and their loved ones. Who will be soon faced countless hours of bull crap. "We may or may not have but at the least two days, to do what we have to do before government agencies start kicking all our doors in, with all kinds of bull shit warrants."

"Yo Sul."

"What's good Hamid?"

"I know one of these names, maybe even two. I'm not sure yet. But this Clif Harper cat.. He's the first name that I know, but what does he have to do with anything this guy is a big time Preacher in my home town. But I think this other witness name Tony Vincent. I'm not quite sure yet, but Tony V is also ringing in my head."

"I'm gonna make a couple phone calls in a few minutes. I heard that name on the news or something. I think someone cut his head off and mailed it to his family, but the rest of his body was left at a hotel or something, to that nature. It was all over the news down my way. If this is the same cat."

"I don't know Hamid.. I think.. Man I don't even know what to say… Please know this.. I love you all, and I'll do anything, and everything to keep you out of harm's way."

"I wish I could turn back the hands of time, on this mess I got you guys in. Real talk.."

"We all must seek Allah, for forgiveness, and the craziest thing is." As Rasul was finishing his sentence, there were two very loud explosions. The first one was the front door folding off its hinges, with wood chips flying everywhere. The second was a flash grenade, which landed almost directly in front of the dining room table that they we're sitting at. The governments S.W.A.T. Teams along with joint D.E.A., A.T.F., and commandoes of New York's finest raided the apartment. Within seconds the penthouse was filled with smoke and different groups of law enforcement.

It took almost three days of deliberation, before the jury came back with a verdict.

The instructions from Judge Walls were strict. Either guilty or not guilty. No hung jury. "Take as much time as you need to do what you have to do, but your gonna come back with a joint agreement."

"Madam Forman." "Have you reached a verdict!"

"Yes.. Your Honor.. We have." We the jury of the United States, 7th District Circuit Court for the State Of Alabama. Find the defendants on count one of conspiracy to Manufacture and Distribute one thousand Kilo grams or more of cocaine. "Guilty."

count two Conspiracy to Interstate Commerce of illegal drug proceeds. "Guilty." and count three of tax evasion "Guilty."

A stunned silence filled the courtroom, and As the Forman started speaking again, the Courtroom erupted with disbelief, mumbling which lead to a few out bursts until the judge quickly took back control of his courtroom. First ordering the on lookers to be removed from the court. Then what made matters even worse, The Assistant United States Attorney Michael Kelly set forth a motion to have all the defendants bail revoked, and remanded not back to the Jefferson County Jail, but sent to the United States Penitentiary Atlanta, detention center unit, pending the sentencing of the defendants. Do to the violent nature, and influence, that may pose a threat to any one of the witnesses.

"Your Honor.. This is papostraous…" I've never in my ten years working as a Florida Assistant Prosecutor, now twenty sum odd years now as a Criminal Defense Attorney, heard of a motion request like this…"

"Now you have counsel!" "Request granted." Judge Walls said then mounted his custom gavel as he stood. "All rise.. The United States District Court for the State of Alabama is now closed" as twelve marshals stepped behind all the defendants, leading them in a single file line out of the courtroom. Each of the defendants holding their heads high, with blank looks in their eyes, were lead to the elevator, then down to the bull pens to be shackled and pressure belted. The thirty five minute ride was a silent one.

All the way to Atlanta. No one spoke a word until the first gate closed, and the second gate opened for the Federal van to pull into the prison.

"Well brothers… Here we go again. Allah knows best about what happened to us earlier today. We all know. We're not guilty of these trumpet up charges. But we are guilty of one thing. When you lock in that cell feeling sorry for yourselves tonight."

"Make two rakats (two full motion prostrations of Islamic prayer to Allah repenting). I love you to death because you're my family but, We're all "Guilty Of Sin!" Shabazz said, from the back seat of the U.S. Marshal's van as he pushed his glasses up the bridge of his noise.

"Damn nat! Which one of y'all brothers, gonna help me explain this ish to my wife Gena?" Tauheed said as he turned his head around from the front row seat. Looking from person to person, as he caught ever one off guard by his comment, and the look on his face. They all had to laugh off the hurt feeling they endured as marshals and the prison guards started escorting them off the van into the Prison to be stripped down of all their rights and clothes, then placed into a federal prison jumpsuit, photo ID'd, then escorted to their new home, (a prison cell).

ACKNOWLEDGEMENTS

My thanks are to Allah first and foremost. When there was no one I had you, behind those walls with no one to talk to in the middle of the night, you never left my side, and now as I watch my life change into so many positive ways I truly thank you. Then to my parents, especially my mother Charlene Miller York Mann, whom never seemed to never give up on me, my father Melvin York, whom if and when I ever needed him he always came thru, to my step-father John W. Mann, I'll never forget the look from your eyes while you were fighting cancer, and the last thing you told me. "Son.. One day you'll be free of that anger inside of you, whether it's physically or mentally, but I'm praying for both for you. Please use that energy as a positive energy and watch how far you go in life. We may have disagreed on a lot of things, but there one thing we both can agree on is that, if you put your mind to it you can achieve almost anything you want. You're a leader by nature, but once you let God take control of your life, the sky will be the limits." To my children, I can't change the past, but everyday above earth we can make it prosperous. And to my youngest brother Charles W. Mann I know I've stressed you out with this book, but at the end of the day I'm greatly thankful. Sibling love is always love ones, thanks to my family and friends who never gave up on me "Diamond Unit for life."

TyMac for Cancer is our non for profit organization started by my brother Ta-tanik York and Marc Victorio. Because we care!

COMING SOON
WE ALL WE GOT !!!

1

"**M**an.. I hope this dude answers his phone." Rasul said as he anticipated, being that the other line was already on its fifth ring. Someone picks up as the recording starts.

"You have a prepaid call from inmate "Rasul" from a United States Federal Penitentiary, if you wish to except this call, you may not click over, use 3 way calling, or call forwarding, failure to these conditions may result in to a termination of this call and disciplinary actions upon the inmate losing his phone privileges. Press "5" if you except this call, "7" if your eject this call, and "9" to block this. As it was saying person.

"Hello."

"Oh man what's good baby boy?"

"Man.. what's really good with you Sul?" "Damn bruh, it's been almost 2 years now, since anybody heard anything from you.. man it's good to hear your voice."

"Listen bro, I put your name on my visiting list, I'm still in Atlanta USP, I really need you to come see me this weekend, our case is going in front of the Court of Appeals for frailer of reading me and Esa our miranda rights, the night we was initially arrested. The judge shot down our motions, in the beginning of our trial, because the prosecution said we were read our rights when we were outside of my building, which the fact of the matter is me and Esa was already in the back of 1 of those trucks, pulling away when they were reading my father and them there rights, feel me."

" So they messed up then."

"Exactly, that's why I need you to come see me. Rondoe listen… I trust no one, especially these phones."

"Say no more big bruh, I'll be there around noon ok." As Ronald was talking the operator voice came across the phone "You have two minutes before this phone disconnects. And that was about a minute and 59 seconds ago, because the phone disconnected.

"911 can I help you."

"Please.. please help us, I need an Ambulance and a paramedic to my home, my husband just came out of the bathroom holding his chest, coughing up blood all over the place."

"Okay Ma'am what you address?"

"It's 702 Oak lane please help, send someone fast. "O God help us?" Now almost screaming out loud into the phone. "What's taking so long, y'all only down the road."

"You have to be a little patient ma'am I'm dispatching emergency vehicles now ok ma'am please stay on the line with us until they get there ok ma'am. Now what's your husband's name".

It's Clifford." "Please God this can't be happening. O my Lord now it sounds like he's chocking on his own blood. "What the heck is taking so long."

Ma'am I'm gonna need you to hold his head slightly up ok, to keep him from further choking, how old is your husband ma'am."

"He's sixty eight years old."

"Does he have any past medical problem, is he on any medication?"

"He takes blood pressure pills. Please lady. O ooh God, please baby hold on, we's don been thru too much for you to give up now, She said crying using her left shoulder and ear to cradle the phone and holding him up with her right hand, as a patrol car and an Ambulance pulled into the drive way.

"Ughhh." Her husband let out a very hard cough which sprayed blood across his wife's face. Rocking him back and forth as the emergency team were now into the house working profusely on him ripping at his shirt to open, while the other Paramedic was trying to start an IV Bag into his forearm, just as an officer was consoling his wife, now sitting on the couch.

"All rise the Honorable Pamela K. Chen Chief Judge for the Second Circuit "United States Court of Appeals for the Eastern District of New York" is now in session. Please be seated."

" Your Honor Paul Mackinary on behalf of the United States Assistant Attorney General's office."

"Good Morning Your Honor, Kenyatta Steward on behalf of the petitioner Rasul York."

"Case number 0317-03- 2255 Motion to Vacate / Correct an illegal sentence, and failure to advise my client of his Miranda Rights upon his arrest. Your Honor as you can read in the motion that's prepared before you, you'll clearly see that my client along with others were clearly the definition of the victim of circumstances clause. My client was not advised of his Miranda rights at any time during his arrest, their whole trial, all the Untied State Attorney proved was, the fact that my client along with other, were convicted felons, and victims of circumstantial evidence. Your Honor, my client along with other said members of "Black Brothers Of Promise" were a Non-Profit organization working out of several states, with not only troubled children but also with local community centers, boy's and girl's clubs, and a slew of cancer awareness organizations throughout this country. I say this to say. "We all have a past, some a lot worse than others, but none of us are perfect. For the betterment of their communities, my client spent countless hours interacting, helping the lives children and Adults, to turn around and be smacked in the face with a life sentence, forrrrrrrrrr."

"Objection Your Honor, the men that's he's speaking so sensitively about, preferably his Client." "The government proved without a doubt, that Rasul York, was nothing less that the master mind and or puppet master of that said organization."

" Sustained Counsel."